Carter-Krall Publishing

Carter-Krall Publishers
42155 Rue Saint Dominique, Suite 207
Stone Mountain, GA 30083

This work of fiction and the novel's story and characters are fictitious. References to actual events, real people living or dead, or to actual locales are intended only to give the literature a sense of reality and authenticity. Certain long-established institutions are mentioned, but the characters in them are wholly imaginary.

Printed in the United States of America
Published by Carter-Krall Publishers First Edition

Cover art by CKP Staff
Typesetting by CKP Staff

Edited by Jennifer Carsen

Catfish Quesadillas/Brian Egeston
ISBN 0-9675505-5-6
Paperback

Library Of Congress Catalog Number
2003091080
First Edition June 2003

Catfish Quesadillas

Brian Egeston

www.brianwrites.com

Carter-Krall Publishing

Dedication

For Jerry D. McCord IV
&
Angus Nile Wilson

I owe both of you so much. Time will never allow me to repay the tremendous debt you have blessed upon me. In hopes that this small token may somehow chip away at my deficit, I thank you for answering all of my phone calls by saying, *Brian, what do you need?* Thanks for:

Feeding me when I am broke, driving me when I have no wheels, taking care of my family while I am away, consoling me when I grieve, asking when I would not tell and most of all, thanks for simply existing.

If friendship is indeed essential to the soul, you have given me enough for this lifetime and the one that will inevitability follow.

Acknowledgments

God, I don't know how you do it, but you continue to put food on the table and keep the lights on. Thank you again and again. Every time I turn around, you're making a way.

My incredible wife. Latise. Thank you for staying by my side during what seems like impossible times. If the world were allowed only one chance at perfect replication, I am certain that you would be the best candidate for DNA cloning. But since it is far-fetched, I'm blessed to have you. One day, I promise, I'll give you every page of the fairy tale.

Thanks to my Dad and siblings JPE dawg and lil' Ollie, aka Jonathan & Christie.

Wonderful test readers, Dejuan Knighton (as always) and the gracious Tracy Justus Berry.

Thanks to my skillful translators Yaneth Boudreau and Nathalye Gutierrez.

Pastor Cynthia L. Hale and the wonderful Ray of Hope Christian church family. Thanks for keeping me lifted up in prayer and your encouraging words.

A wonderful thanks to all the bookclubs and organizations that continue to welcome me with open arms and kitchens. I'd fill the entire book with names if I listed them all. Thanks to Angela and the Huntsville, Alabama crew; Tonya and the Roanoke, Virginia gang. A special thanks to

Shelly and the entire Quad Cities community. Thanks for making me feel like a star and a cousin.

Thanks to the educational facilities that have allowed me to come in and lecture to your young minds. Georgia Perimeter, Blackwell College, Piccowaxen Middle School, Inman Middle School.

Thanks to St. John Flynn and Art Silverman, Dekalb Neighbor, Black Issues Book Review, Midwest Book Review, QBR (Max and Nancey), Creative Loafing, Rolling Out Magazine, AALBC.com, Mosaicbooks.com, Booking Matters and Shunda Blocker, my fellow faith walker.

Thanks to the great bookstores that give me shelf space. Maleta, you're the best and thanks for looking out for me. Thanks to Mardessa Smith and your wonderful skills. Thanks to Tonya Evans and the staff at EBE Law for keeping me on the straight and narrow.

A special thanks to the entire Les chateaux subdivision. My neighbors and friends. I'll start paying my association dues on time, I promise.

Thanks to the Williams and Hill families for your painful and wonderful testimonies. Through your faith and your victory, I keep marching on.

Thanks to my fraternity brothers who exercise patience by allowing me to disappear from action for months at a time so that I can struggle and create. Thanks for not giving up on me and thanks for never leaving me or thinking of leaving me.

Thanks to the cities of Little Rock and Hope, Arkansas. I will always remember the embracing love that so many people gave during my mother's passing. It blessed me more than you will ever know.

Thanks to the Egeston, Nash, Searles, and Hadley families. Whew! Four family reunions, couldn't ask for more than that. Thanks for instant and long-lasting love.

Thanks to my proud writing organizations—Black Writers Alliance, Atlanta Black Writers, Prolific Writers, Village Writers Group, Georgia Writers. Geri, I'm gonna help. I promise!

And thanks to the readers and fans of Whippins, Switches & Peach Cobbler and Granddaddy's Dirt. As I continue to evolve as a writer, my only wish is that you push me each time to write better, to tell bolder stories and to write for your grandchildren and your grandchildren's children.

Special thanks to my writer buddies and family. Thanks for keeping on the battlefield.

I know I've forgotten someone somewhere somehow. If it's you, please accept my deepest apologies. Please e-mail me and I'll get you in the next book...I promise.

Table of Contents

Dekalb County, Georgia
2003

Chapter One

Toxic Super Size

Two men stood in the large silver box, lips billowing curls of cold breath, hands clutching small bags of poison.

"Escoge el pollo. Todos Estaran muy enfermos," said one, pointing to a stack of boxes inside the walk-in refrigerator.

The other took his suggestion and camouflaged the particles in the marinated chicken.

"Mas. Mas."

"More?"

"Si. Mas. Estan muy enfermos."

"I'm not tryin' to kill nobody. Just make 'em sick," he said, gesturing a hand slitting his own throat.

"Ellos no moren, para muy enfermos."

The two men had been hiding in the restroom since an hour before closing time. It seemed a much better plan than breaking in through the back kitchen and hoping the burglar alarm decals were lies. It was cold in the restaurant's refrigerator and nerves made lungs work faster, blood thrust harder. Their consciences pricked at the backs of their necks. The gringo swiped at the poultry quickly, haphazardly. Was there a proper method for dispensing poison? If there was, he didn't know it and didn't care. He just wanted a few people to feel slightly ill. Just sick enough to reconsider. His Spanish-speaking compadre had been hired as a Judas lookout. He was a former employee who knew the restaurant and could maneuver through it in the dark.

After tainting the last box, they took the cases out of the refrigerator so that the food would sit out all night at room temperature, breeding bacteria to mingle with the poison. The men planned to babysit the tampered poultry all night and then return it to the refrigerator as the sun came up. Too nervous to sleep and too anxious to sit still, the gringo roamed around the restaurant. He was careful not to be seen by headlights shining through the front windows as he groped his way around in the dark.

There was just enough light for him to faintly make out the pictures on the wall. Leaning to one side trying to get a better reflection from the streetlights, he saw families in the frames hanging on the walls. Perhaps they were generations of immigrants and ancestors. Elderly people were sitting, holding infants. Young adults looked over the old shoulders, cradling newborn bodies. Within the frames were bloodlines of survivors, fighters, and benefactors. He felt their eyes on him as he crept around the tables.

During the day, this room was filled with exuberant eaters, consumers of trendy ethnic dishes. Several restaurants like this had often closed before they'd opened—in some cases even before the "Grand Opening" sign had been ordered. But not this one. This one was unbelievably successful. Too successful. Something would have to be done in order to ensure the existence of competitors. The entrepreneurial food chain needed an adjustment, the man thought.

But as time collided with destiny and darkness was relieved by light, he began to regret what he'd done. It seemed as though the smiling faces were already in the building. He could see the results of his actions. He himself began to feel slightly ill, thinking of what was about to transpire and rushed toward the walk-in to right his wrong. He was going to throw out the contaminated food and run home. His accomplice was propped up against the wall, nodding with a light sleep. The cases of chicken they'd left out on the counter were gone. He kicked his sleeping partner, startling him awake. With appalling Spanish, he asked him about the food.

"Uh... donday is polo?"

"Ahi," he replied pointing to the cooler. He'd placed the food back into the unit when the sun began to peek over the horizon. The two men went back and forth, talking and interpreting. The Spanish to English translation was arduous — the men were unknowingly telling each other that the cold chicken was feeling bad. They nodded heads in agreement, realizing that neither knew what the other wanted.

The intruder decided that his actions would speak clearly. He approached the refrigerator door, to remove the cases of food and toss them in the garbage. Then his partner would see that he was sorry for what he'd done. But when he yanked on the handle, a spine-numbing pulse jolted through his body. The door was locked. He pulled the handle again, to no avail. He began jerking the handle repeatedly, like a jackhammer pounding away on a surface it would never break.

"Why's the door locked!" he asked, hoping that his partner would understand. If not, the face-contorting fear would certainly give him a clue.

"Is lock," the man replied, with infomercial-English.

"I know it's locked! But why is it locked! How can it be locked now, if it wasn't locked when we came in? What's really goin' on up in here! You tryin' to get me sent up or somethin'! If I get caught, then..." He stopped, realizing the tirade was useless. What little the man did understand was surely lost in the ferocious delivery.

"Yo no se," the man replied, explaining that he did not know. He shook his head to help the gringo understand the message.

"We gotta get this door open. We made a mistake, bruh. Get the polos! Get the polos! Compren-day?"

"Si. El pollos es malo. Is bad."

"I know it's bad. That's why I wanna get 'em out. Get polo out!"

The intruder pulled the door and resumed the futile jackhammer yanking. Repetitive noises and heavy breathing joined in harmony with his shouts. Shouts of regret, shouts of fear, shouts of what was to come in this place later today. Suddenly there was another sound coming from the back door. The men froze when they heard keys jingling and meshing with a lock. The sounds bounced sharp and crisp against the hard surfaces of the room. A steel bolt sliding open, a twisting doorknob, a squeaking hinge. The door swung open and they heard someone whistling. It was a carefree tune of some catchy song heard on the radio that would remain in the whistler's head until a better one took its place. Making music as though today had the potential to become the world's best date yet.

The whistler walked from the back and began turning on lights, making her way to the front registers. Once she was a safe distance away, the two men darted for the exit when suddenly the sounds started again. The bolt, the hinge, the opening door. Another worker was making his way in through the back. The two men ducked behind a rack of bread just next to the doorway. They watched with bucked eyes, held breath, and erratic hearts. As the second worker entered, they saw him move immediately towards the cooler. They heard the locked handle being tugged a few times.

The man shouted to the front, "Maria. La purta es locked again. ¿Cuando vas a arreglar la nevera?"

"Hector!" she yelled back. "Speak English. You won't get better unless you use it every day, all the time."

He pulled the handle once again, sighing in frustration with the English and the stubborn door.

"I say, dee door es lock again. We need get dee door fixed-ed."

"I'll talk to Juan about it when he comes from the meeting today. You have to shake the handle and push it until it pops open."

Hector did as she instructed and resumed the now-familiar jackhammering.

Behind the bread rack, the intruders listened to the shaking and then heard the fateful sound of an airtight seal being released as the cooler's door opened. The two opened the back door and fled towards Memorial Drive under the now dimly lit skies of Stone Mountain, Georgia. They hoped that the brief refrigeration of the chicken would be enough to save the hundreds of customers who would enter the La Familia restaurant over the next sixteen hours.

Chapter Two

Million Dollar Mayhem

Monday morning, there was a kaleidoscope of people brightening an office filled with dark furniture. There was a man so dark he was blurple (black and purple), two sun-baked bronze men, a small yellow-beige woman, and a female entrepreneur the color of coffee touched with cream. All had convened to discuss emerald colored paper.

"Usted es un pez gordo en su compania pero tambien es un buen jefe. Le estoy muy a gradcido."

"What did he say?" asked Karen Batch, a small business consultant.

"He says you are big wig in your company but you are good boss. He is very grateful to you," replied Juan Santos, translating for his business partner and fighting his own accent.

"Yeah that goes for me too, Karen. We appreciate what you doin' for our businesses and the community," said Randall Harvey.

"Tank you velly much," added Juliet Lee.

"Again, it's my pleasure," said Karen. "Whoever gets the million-dollar grant will be able to improve their business and begin to change the face of Memorial Drive. We want DeKalb county to be a corner stone for community revitalization. Although we're in Stone Mountain, we want to take this improvement to Decatur, Lithonia, Clarkston, and all of the other cities that make up metro Atlanta. But I must reiterate—it's strictly up to you who will receive the grant. Each of you has done very well in the first phases of the business evaluation, but when the mystery shoppers come, and they will come soon, the final decision will be based solely on their scores. So it's all in your hands. Here's a chance to put your past behind you and move forward with positive change. Understand? Good. Now if you'll excuse me, I've got to get ready for a meeting."

The small crowd began moving toward the door. Those still trying to cross the language barrier noticed the others were leaving and followed the lead. All except for Randall. Instead, he held the door open for all the others. He wanted to steal a few moments alone with Karen.

Randall was the proprietor of a profitable yet struggling empire. He owned Fish Nets, a small, delectable seafood restaurant. Randall dreamed of someday having a sign out front that read *Harvey & Sons*. A family pride, a legacy that would carry on for generations. But Randall's family legacy suffered from too many bad ideas disguising themselves as business ventures. His eldest son, Corey, was a 21-year-old business failure in capitalist's clothing.

The energy and determination of Randall's first-born never seemed to match his ingenuity. Despite the eighteen cell phone dealers within a five-mile radius, Corey decided to open up number nineteen. Although the strip was littered with car detailers, Corey was adamant that he could wash cars better than the five others pumping suds and water right across the street. The fragrance store was the only venture that didn't lose money every single week. But that branch of the family business was beginning to wilt as well. Corey stuffed his wallet with business cards from each of the "subsidiaries," as he liked to call them. His conglomeration's name was *Holla If Ya Hear Me, Inc.* — his attempt at youthfully misplaced exuberance.

Randall glowed with pride each time Corey ran into the office with another of his well-articulated ideas. He urged his son to build a business model and devise a business plan — something Randall himself had never taken the time to do, perhaps his greatest downfall. But he preached the message to his son hoping the boy could learn from his mistakes. The headstrong son paid him no mind, arguing that by the time he'd finished with the red tape, as he called it, someone else would have taken his market share. *As if there were a market share for another poorly organized and managed Black business*, thought Randall.

Randall finally stopped his son's ambition when he refused to give him capital for his latest brainstorm — a hot wing stand. There were at least fifty local wing shacks spewing grease fumes into the community and Randall was dead set against the idea of one more. Father and son argued for days until Randall drove Corey around for half an hour and demanded that he count the trailers masquerading as restaurants. Corey changed his mind about the idea when he'd lost count of all the wing shacks and they'd been driving for only fifteen minutes. While sitting at a red light, Corey tried to recall if Radical Right Wings was shack number twenty-three — or was it Wing My Bell or Hair Wigs & Hot Wings? It was the thought of chicken wings and hair that ultimately made him lose count — and his appetite.

He returned home with a new zeal for improving and growing the family seafood restaurant, which he'd deemed his own personal future empire. Randall confided to Corey that their establishment was suffering and in desperate need of a miracle. A million-dollar miracle. Randall explained that the grant was their only chance of survival. Somehow other businesses had come to the area and figured out how to succeed faster and with seemingly fewer resources.

Randall stood there, lost in his thoughts, holding the door open for the others ,thinking of a way out of his impending failure. Suddenly, he realized he was alone in the room with Karen Batch.

"Uh, Karen. I wonder if I could talk to you for a moment."

The professional woman glanced strangely at him, then at her watch—having already announced that the meeting was over.

"Well, make it quick. I've got another meeting in five minutes."

"Yes, ma'am. I will."

"Please, cut out that ma'am' stuff. I could be your daughter."

"Well, I was wonderin' if you had any advice, you know, business advice that might help out for the evaluations. My place has been around for a long time and it would be a shame if the only Black business bein' evaluated didn't uh...you know...Well, if we had to close down because our competitors won. And Lord knows they ain't got the community's best interest in mind. If you got any advice, I'd greatly appreciate it. In fact if you have any...y'know, trainin', I would gladly pay...."

"Stop right there, Mr. Harvey." Her voice was sharp. "I tell you what, stop right there. Back up and erase everything you just said. I am certain you aren't implying that you're trying to purchase knowledge that might give an advantage during this evaluation."

With eyebrows raised, Karen was moving from poised to pissed. "I'll give you some advice, all right. Get outta my office talkin' that nonsense. And the next piece of advice I'll give you is get back to that restaurant and fix yo' problems. 'Cause I'll tell you one thing. I don't know how you got this far, but you won't survive the mystery shoppers.

"Mr. Harvey, I've been to your restaurant — several times. And the food is good. But it's not good enough to make up for the service. I have some small level of tolerance, but the mystery shoppers will cut you to shreds for some of the things that go on in your establishment. Do you know that someone there had the *nerve* to tell me...never mind." She shook her head and looked Randall squarely in the eye. "Mr. Harvey, fix your problems. That's the advice I can give you. And I mean fix them all. And fix them quick."

"Why you actin' like this? We supposed to be helpin' each other. Every time somebody Black —"

"Nope. You can stop right there. I won't even listen to anything else. Don't expect me to respond, because I won't. Have a good day, Mr. Harvey, and fix your problems. Starting with that disaster that you call a host or register operator." Randall was appalled. He wanted so badly to leave in a fury, slamming the door off its hinges. But civility and common sense prevailed, and he took his leave quietly. He carefully closed the office door as he left.

He had the overwhelming desire to immediately return to his restaurant and observe the disaster Karen had mentioned. His patrons did indeed call her a cashier, along with a few other vulgar nouns. To Randall, however, she was simply — a daughter.

Chapter Three

Customer Disservice

"Then go somewhere else if you want trout. I told you we ain't got no mo'!"

"But haven't you only been open for about three hours...Veronica," a customer said, squinting to read the faded name on the badge. "How could you have run out that fast?" Monday's lunch crowd was always a feisty group, reluctant to get back in the routine of yet another week.

"I'm through talkin' to you. Get out the line. I got mo' customers to take care of. Who next?" The feisty hostess cackled and reached next to the register for her drink, an enormous tub of Coke. She slurped on the straw, which was saturated with lipstick. Obviously working through whatever lunch break she would miss, she swiped a french fry from her snack stash and began chomping while the next customer ordered.

Veronica momentarily dropped her fries and began smacking her own head with a skull-shaking ferocity.

"Oooh, my head is itchin'!" she said, then turned to the customer who had just ordered. "Now, you said a whitin' sandwich with french fries and a Coke?" She gingerly pressed the register keys with her fake fingernails. Veronica dared not chip her freshly manicured masterpieces of swirling blue and orange polish. Each nail had a dollar amount painted on it. The pinky of her left hand started with one hundred dollars and the pinky of her right hand ended with one thousand dollars. When men would inquire about the nails, she simply stated that she was worth more and more each day and they would have to pay if they wanted to play.

Her nails were done weekly at Lee's Nail Salon. There were more nail technicians working there than at Nikki's Nails, the Black-owned nail shop. And the determining factor—the prices were much cheaper. No matter what type of promotion Nikki's Nails ran, Lee's Nails would always counter with a better deal.

"No! I asked for a whiting dinner with an iced tea," said the agitated customer. *"You're* the one eating french fries and drinking a Coke. All while serving customers, I might add."

"Hold on missy. Who you think you talkin' to? I ain't got to serve you at all. You can walk yo' a—"

"Ma'am, we'll get that order right out to you. Sorry for the inconvenience." Randall had caught the beginning of the spectacle and knew he would have to step in, as he always did. "Jessie, would you take over the register for your sister?"

"Okay, Pops." Jessie, 16 years old, was Randall's youngest. He wolfed down the last bite of his lunch, washed it away with a swallow of water, and tossed his carryout bag in the trash. Jessie stepped behind the register and flashed an enthusiastic smile.

"I'm sorry you had to wait. How can I help you?" His warm spirit splashed the customer with the refreshing reality that she was important and should be treated as such. The smiling young man plowed through the order and served the remaining customers with expedient and pleasant service.

Meanwhile, Randall walked his daughter to the back of the store and held another consultation. He hoped that this one would prove more effective than all of the others he seemed to have with her each week.

"Babygirl, is everything all right?"

"Nawh, everything ain't all right! You heard how that wench was talkin' to me. I'm tired of these people treatin' me like I'm trash."

"Veronica, I know you upset, baby. But people only gonna give back what you give 'em. If you nasty to 'em, then they'll be nasty right back."

"So you sayin' it was my fault that lady treated me like she wanted me to put my foot up her crack?"

"Well, you gotta ask yourself that question. I mean, you was eatin' on the front line, like I asked you not to."

"I might not get a break today, Daddy! Am I'm supposed to starve so I can wait on some disrespectful people?"

"You know as well as I do that you won't starve. Besides, we can't just talk to customers any way we want to. They pay the bills and your salary, too."

"I don't care what they do. That woman can't talk to me any way she want to."

"Honey, sometimes you got to be a little bit more forgiving with some customers."

"No I don't. If I don't want to put up with that mess, I ain't *got* to do nothin'."

"What would happen if she stopped comin' here to eat and told all her friends not to come here?"

"To hell wit' all of 'em!"

"Then what would we do about money?"

"Huh, what you talkin' about?"

"If we don't have customers, how we gon' stay in business? How we gon' pay for the house note and get those nails done every week?"

"Aw, Daddy, you can't—"

Suddenly, an enormous crash boomed through the restaurant.

"Help! Get some help out here!"

34

Randall's first thought was that there was a fight. He hoped that his son hadn't hit one of the customers or worse—a mystery shopper.

"He's choking!" someone yelled. Randall rushed to the front, thinking that this was the last day of his business. The word would get out that the cashiers were rude and the food choked people. Reporters would show up after the police arrived and his restaurant would be all over the news, with bad publicity. Today however, there would be no police, only an ambulance.

When Randall reached the front counter, there was indeed someone struggling to breathe. His son was on the floor convulsing. Saliva foamed around his lips and ran down the side of his face. His head jerked violently, slamming against the tile floor.

"Somebody call 911!" Randall shouted as he held his son. He held the boy like he had many years ago when Jessie had fallen and scraped his knee, or bumped his head. He held him the way he'd held all of his children at one time or another. It was all he knew how to do. Jessie continued to convulse in his arms. Veronica stood beside them, her eyes wide.

"Clear the way!" a team of paramedics who had come in on their lunch break pushed through the small crowd. They rushed to the boy and performed their duties precisely, almost mechanically. While one kept Jessie from swallowing his tongue, the other ran to the ambulance and retrieved the stretcher.

"What's wrong with him? Why is he doin' this?" Randall shouted.

"It's a seizure," said one of the paramedics. "Has this happened before? Is he epileptic?"

"No. Ain't nothin' wrong with my son. He's always had good health."

"We're gonna take him to the hospital. You might want to ride along with us."

The other paramedic returned with the stretcher. Corey had pulled up in front of the restaurant just as the paramedic darted out. He knew something was wrong. He followed the stretcher inside asking questions with each step.

"Daddy, what's wrong?" Corey yelled.

"We don't know, son, your brother's had a seizure. We're about to go to the hospital now."

"A seizure? How? Why?"

"I don't know, Corey. Guess we'll find out at the hospital," Randall said calmly, trying to mask his panic.

"Was he doing anything before this happened?" One of the paramedics turned to Veronica.

"I don't know. We was in the back talkin'," Veronica replied. She was hysterical. Her little brother seemed to be fighting with death and there was nothing she could do to help him.

"He had just finished eating something," a customer said. It was the woman who'd waited at the register while Jessie took over for Veronica.

"He ate somethin' from here?" Randall asked, in shock. He instantly thought of the fallout from his own son becoming ill by the food from the family restaurant.

"No. I think he was eating something out of a red bag," she said.

Veronica looked in a can behind the counter. It was where she always threw her garbage after she'd finished eating her front line contraband. She reached into the small garbage can and pulled out a crumpled red bag.

"Is this what he was eating from?" asked the paramedic.

"Yeah, that's it," the customer said.

"We'd better take that with us, just in case," said Randall.

Veronica handed the bag to her father. Corey looked on with paralyzing fear and vindictive anger as he saw the large white letters: La Familia Restaurant.

Chapter Four

The Breakout Outbreak

Food poisoning was the breaking story on the evening news. An immediate connection had been made with the discovery of the bag containing Corey's leftover chicken quesadillas, La Familia's signature dish. Five other patients—with milder but similar symptoms—had all reported eating lunch at La Familia. At six-thirty, a live update of the food poisoning case was broadcast by a reporter standing in front of the DeKalb Medical Center. And that's when the entire city and surrounding areas—a total of five million people—found out about the popular Mexican restaurant on Memorial Drive.

At seven o'clock, someone shot-put a red brick through La Familia's large plate glass window. The weapon found no casualties in the unusually deserted dining room. An angry moron venting emotions or perhaps someone waiting for an opportunity to be moronic. The shot-putter became a sprinter upon seeing a large truck squeal into the restaurant's parking lot.

Poles and ladders were piled into the truck's bed, along with two men; three other men were squished into the truck's cab. Five of them. They always traveled five deep. On the door panels were the words *Santos Services. Plumbing, Carpeting, Building, Masonry. Se Hablo Espanol.* The more men in the truck, the more family members got the opportunity to work. When more people worked, the jobs were done faster. When jobs were done faster, they could start on other projects while other companies over-extended their stay on job sites. Each project completed meant more experience gained. With more experience, they would build their reputation. The quintet jumped from the truck and quickly began measuring the broken pane.

More people had been rushed to the hospital, all with varied and unusual symptoms: excess salivating, foaming at the mouth, muscle spasms, labored breathing, numbed legs. Flashing ambulance lights pounded the evening dusk while drivers scattered their cars in the hospital parking lots with no concern for the carefully painted white parking lines. People who had eaten at La Familia that day—and even some who'd eaten there two days prior—were piling into the unsuspecting emergency room.

Locals craving Mexican food that night decided to turn elsewhere to satisfy their south-of-the-border urges. Taco Bell received an unusual surge of business that evening. People pulling up to the drive-thru menu board asked jokingly, "*Your* food isn't poisonous, is it?"

Word spread throughout the city with the speed of a forest fire, but on Memorial Drive the news blazed through with the force of a flame-thrower. Within a matter of hours, residents were talking about *that Mexican place*. The consensus amongst the community was that the restaurant had caused an epidemic. But then they saw the unfolding drama on the eleven o'clock news report.

Juan Santos stood at the front of his restaurant, beaming in spotlights from television cameras and besieged from an array of microphones in his face. A few bumped his nose and one even scratched his clean-shaven chin. As best he could, the man answered questions machine-gunned by the reporters.

"Mr. Santos, who—"

"Mr. Santos, over here!"

"Sir, tell us why—"

"Mr. Santos, what can you tell us about the food poisoning accusations connected to your restaurant?" One of the media hounds finally broke through.

Juan was defensive. "This is not something that could happen in, eh, my restaurant."

"But sir, there are dozens of people at DeKalb Medical Center all experiencing the same symptoms—the only thing they have in common is that they ate here within the last few days. How do you explain that?"

"I have no, eh, explain for dat. But I can tell you, my restaurant is very clean."

"Mr. Santos—"

"Mr. Santos. Over here, can you—"

"What will your establishment do differently in the future to prevent this from happening?"

"We will do de same thing we always do. Nothing will, eh, nothing will change."

"But Mr. Santos, don't you think other people might be in danger if you don't change your sanitation habits?"

"No." Santos replied with firm conviction.

The reporters, surprised, began to mumble about the one word refusal. Others composed copious notes while a few more prodded even deeper.

"Mr. Santos, why won't you make changes?"

Suddenly, Juan held up a stack of yellow papers for the cameras and reporters to see. He'd been waiting for just the right moment.

"Because this say my restaurant is clean. Look at these, eh, scores. All of you, look at them. January twelve, three year ago, one hundred—perfect score. Marsh, eh, twenty-nine, three year ago—perfect score.

Look, put your camera here," he said with a righteous haughtiness. "July two, one year ago—perfect score. Look, last month perfect score!"

The stack of papers was thick and each report from the county board of health was a replica of perfection. Every inspection had resulted in the best possible score—one hundred. And as the live cameras kept rolling, those watching knew, just as Juan Santos did, that something was foul.

Anxious to exonerate himself in the instantaneous court of public perception, Juan Santos began handing out his perfect scores.

"Here, please take one," he repeated to each reporter. "Here, please, eh, take one. Tell de news that La Familia is clean and this could not happen in my restaurant." The reporters unleashed another barrage of questions.

"Mr. Santos!"

"Mr. Santos, what do—"

"How do you feel about—"

"Mr. Santos, do you suspect sabotage? Could someone have intentionally poisoned your food? Do you think an employee did it?"

Santos whipped his head towards the direction of the inquiry. He looked into the blinding light with piercing eyes and scorned them all.

"Never! La Familia is family. Family does not do this to a business! Every member of my family works hard here. We are here for opportunity! To make better way for more families to come from Mexico! Don't you ever accuse my family of this! No more questions."

He turned and rushed back towards the restaurant to help the men repairing the window as more inquisitions were futilely cast toward his back.

The television reporter who'd broken the story at the hospital turned to the camera .

"And there you have it, Brenda. As you just witnessed..." She glanced down at her notes to recall the name. "Mr. Juan Santos, owner of La Familia here on Memorial Drive, claims that there is no way this could have happened at his restaurant. He gave members of the media his board of health results and it seems that each one is a perfect score. But he seemed very upset when someone brought up the idea of sabotage. I have a feeling we'll be hearing more developments on this story." She wrapped up the broadcast and waited for the live feed to clear.

Juan stopped the window repair to vent his frustration over the questions he'd been asked. The men, all Juan's family members, listened intently.

One of the men, a wiring expert, interrupted Juan. He'd just crossed the border a few months earlier and was struggling with the language.

"I, eh, push-ed dee can at dee back."

"What?" Juan asked. He insisted that everyone speak English at all times. If they were to exist and thrive here, then communicating was key — most of the time.

"Dee back, es a cannon," the man replied holding his hands in front of his face and moving one finger up and down as though he were pressing a button.

"Espanol," Juan finally relented.

"La semana pasada yo puse una camara escondida alta atras."

"What! Where? Show me! Now!"

The men rushed to the back of the restaurant and the wiring expert pointed out his handiwork. A hidden video camera.

Chapter Five

Bulk Business

The next morning, Juliet Lee was one of the many people discussing yesterday's unfolding events. It was Tuesday, which meant that she had to supervise the incoming product shipments for her store, Black Beauty. The shop was a mega-beauty supply store that primarily sold hair care products for Blacks. From hair curlers to perm chemicals, Black Beauty boasted the best prices in the metropolitan Atlanta area. Products often fell from the shelves because there was such an abundance of stock. Juliet insisted that her employees—who were also her family members—keep the goods in plain view for the customer. *If the customer can't see it, the customer can't buy it,* she often professed.

There was a very small storage space in the back of the building, but most of the inventory was on the floor. It was extremely rare that a customer could not find what they wanted in Black Beauty. Customers almost never heard the phrase, We *just ran out of that, we'll have some in next week.*

Raja Distribution was a hub for many small businesses receiving products for their stores. It was where Juliet received her products. Tech-Tron Systems, a Chinese-owned computer shop, and Talk-Time, the largest cell phone dealership on Memorial Drive, received all of their products at Raja's, also.

The 100,000-square foot warehouse, open twenty-four hours, was a small city in and of itself. Forklifts sped across the floor carrying pallets stacked with boxes. After a few accidents, Raja was forced to hire a person dedicated to directing forklift traffic. At any given hour, twelve forklifts raced back and forth, loading and unloading.

Businesses like Black Beauty and Tech-Tron leased space at Raja's to store the massive amounts of products they received each month. It was how Juliet was able to always have product available. In previous years, she'd had products shipped overnight and found that the shipping costs were absorbing her profit margin. Then she decided to run her business like a family — keeping everything close.

"Did you hear about that Mexican place last night on the news?" a woman standing in line behind Juliet asked.

"Yes I hear. It was really bad for those people," she responded.

The woman behind Juliet, a beautiful heavyset woman with midnight skin, was a business owner herself. She was there to pick up a new piece of equipment for her salon.

It was Juliet's turn to approach the window. "Hi, Rasha. How you?"

"Juliet, nice to see you again. How's business?"

"It fine. Thank you. How much I have, today?"

"Oh very much! Today you receive seventeen pallets. Five thousand pounds of products. Business is very good, yes?" asked Rasha.

"Yes, thank you. You keep four thousand pound at warehouse and I send truck to pick up one thousand pound. Okay?"

"Sure, that's fine." The woman in the window gave Juliet a sheet of paper listing all of the products that had been delivered. "Have a nice day. Tell your family hello."

"Yes, fine. Thank you."

Juliet walked out the door, making notes on the paper. She was figuring out where the products would be sent based on the inventory taken during the week. After checking items halfway down the list, she was approached by the woman who had been standing behind her in line.

"Excuse me. I don't mean to be rude, but did that lady say you had five thousand pounds of somethin'?"

"Yes."

"Chile, what kinda business you got? Where you put all that stuff?"

Juliet covered her mouth and gave a modest laugh at the question. "It not all mine. Not all for my store. It all for many stores owned by friends and family. We have group of twenty store in city and we order at same time together and use one name to order all product. It much cheap to do that way."

"Really! Twenty stores. All twenty Chinese restaurants? Is that how y'all be given all that food away at them lunch buffets? Girl, I be tearin' up some egg rolls. You don't own the Chinese place next to the car wash, do you? I eat there all the time 'cause I own that little hair salon and beauty supply place across the street. If that's you or your people, let me know. I'll send all my clients over there. Us minorities gotta help each other, if you know what I mean."

Juliet laughed harder at the verbose woman. "No. No restaurants. We have group of stores for hair. We have these kind products," Juliet said pointing to the sheet.

The nosy woman looked on as Juliet pointed at the huge inventory.

Juliet began rattling off the names. "African oil, Isoplus condition—"

"Wait a minute," the lady exclaimed. "This is stuff that I use. I sell it too. You got a case of perm care for eight dollars? A case cost me thirteen dollars. Who you buyin' this stuff from?"

"We buy from distributor."

"I do too, but I don't get it for eight dollars a case. And what is this? No lye relaxer for eighty-six cents each! I pay two dollars apiece for this! What the hell is this! What kinda business you got, lady, a bootleg hair salon?"

"What is bootleg mean? Is like shoe store? My cousin have shoe store. My store is Black Beauty. It on Memorial. If you no live close you can visit one of—"

"Black Beauty! *You* own that store? I ought knock yo' slanted eyes open!" the insensitive woman yelled. Her proclamation of minority unity had been destroyed. "You know how many people you done put out of business? We can't hardly sell nothin' with y'all cuttin' them prices so low. What the hell wrong wit' chu? I got fifteen girlfriends with shops all over the city and we can't make no money off hair care stuff 'cause every other heifer come through the door got mess they done already bought from Black Beauty. Look at you. Ain't nothin' Black about you! Why don't you open up a store called Yellow Fever or somethin'. You got some nerve."

Juliet stood swimming in the tongue tirade, struggling to understand everything the woman was saying. But she clearly understood every word of the next statement.

"Black people want to shop at Black businesses. You ain't Black! Go back to China, you crazy bat!"

Juliet gasped. She'd been insulted like this before and always refrained from trading verbal blows. But this time she couldn't hold back. "I have many Black customer! They like my store! My store get bigger! You no talk to me like that!"

"What...you...I...wait til...Who the hell do you think?" the woman said, readying herself for war. She was unclasping one of her earrings just as a large warehouse security guard walked over and stepped between them.

"Is there a problem here, ladies?" He was a mountain of a man, his shirt buttons holding on for dear life. One large sigh and they might become bullets.

"She try attack me. She insult," said Juliet Lee, pointing.

"Ain't nobody attacked you, yet! If I attacked you, you'd be bleedin'." She began to remove her other earring.

"All right, all right," the guard said. "You get in your car, and ma'am, you get in your car. Then we'll all have a nice day."

"You all go away. We make you soon. You too lazy. You see. We close you all down," Juliet lashed. Her mild temper had erupted.

"What you say! Trick, I'll knock the..." the lady replied, taking a swing in Juliet's direction. It was cut short by the swollen guard's bulk and his meaty outstretched arm.

"Hey! Am I not speaking clearly enough or do you need the police to say it? Get in your cars and leave!"

The guard became more aggressive as the two attracted more attention from onlookers.

"Tell her! She the one keep on talkin'!"

"I'm telling both of you. Leave!"

"I leave now!" Juliet said, furious. She walked to her car with frantic strides. When she was a safe distance away, Juliet yelled back, "My family close you all down!"

Chapter Six

Daring Demands

By early Tuesday afternoon, Randall wanted revenge. He wanted someone to pay for what had happened to his son. He wanted prosperity in exchange for his suffering. The million-dollar grant seemed much more meaningful than it had a few days ago, now Randall wanted it—immediately. He knew it was irrational, but he viewed it as a payback for what had happened to his son.

Jessie was still in a light coma, but he was well cared for by the hospital staff and had visitors 'round the clock. Randall had been there since Jessie's admission and needed a break. The restaurant was in the hands of Corey and Veronica, which made him somewhat anxious to get back and check on things.

Corey called every hour, asking about his brother's condition and giving Randall updates on the restaurant. It was Corey's first experience with the addictive power of being in control.

Other victims were being released after stomach pumpings and large doses of antibiotics. The doctors told Randall they weren't sure why Corey'd had such a sudden and violent reaction to the possible contamination, but speculated that it was because he may have consumed an extremely large amount of whatever had infected everyone else. It was then that Randall left the hospital in a rage. He didn't care that Karen Batch was a professional woman with a hectic schedule, nor that he didn't have an appointment. She would see him immediately because he wouldn't stop at the receptionist's desk. Instead, he would barge into her office and make his demands.

"I want those people taken off that damn list for the grant, right now!" Randall exclaimed as Karen sat and watched in disbelief. The receptionist followed a few seconds later, her face twisted with a look of anger.

"Let me give you a call later. I have a security issue here," Karen said placing the phone on its hook.

Randall tensed at the mention of security. Karen rose from her seat and Randall took a few steps backwards.

"Linda, thank you. Could you leave us alone for a few minutes?" The receptionist straightened her ruffled clothes and gave Randall a scornful look as she exited.

Karen closed the door and gracefully walked back to her desk.

"How's your son doing, Mr. Harvey?"

Her kind demeanor was confusing.

"He in a coma! How da hell you *think* he doin'!" exclaimed Randall.

"That was a very unfortunate incident. We all..."

"You damn right it was unfortunate! Those people runnin' a nasty place of business and they need to be shut down! Ain't no way that restaurant should be up for any kinda grant!"

"I understand your frustration, Mr. Harvey, and I've already begun taking steps in that direction."

"Huh? You already kicked them out of the runnin'?" Randall asked. Karen's statement eased his rampage.

"No, not exactly. What I have done is made some phone calls and checked out their history. I did that even before we offered the grant consideration."

"What that got to do with anything?" asked Randall.

"A lot, actually. Do you recall the lowest score you've ever received from the Board of Health?"

"Huh? Who remembers that kinda stuff? If anything, that's the score I wanna forget."

"Do you know the lowest score La Familia has ever received?"

"I don't know and I don't care. All I know is they need to be taken off the grant thing."

"One hundred, Mr. Harvey. La Familia has been in business for seven years and has never had a score less than one hundred. That's a perfect score."

"So, what that mean?"

"It means, it doesn't make sense for an establishment with a record such as that to have a food contamination problem."

"You on they side now? Is that it?"

"Mr. Harvey." Karen remained calm. She glanced down at her desk and saw her daily affirmation printed on a calendar. *Today I will be in control and remain in control of all of my emotions.* She released a sigh of frustration, then continued. "I have no personal interest in this grant award, nor do I have anything to profit or gain from any of this. My only interest is that the grant is awarded in complete fairness. And you have to realize, as do the police, that this doesn't make sense."

"What police? What they got to do with this?"

"The police, along with the Board of Health, are looking into foul play on this incident. That's who I was talking to before you interrupted."

"What! That's crazy. What they lookin' for?"

"I can only assume sabotage, Mr. Harvey. I'm sure they will be contacting you also."

"Contactin' me? For what? My place ain't got nothin' to do with this. My boy is layin' in a coma at the hospital from some nasty Mexican place that need to be taken off the grant and then closed down! I ain't got nothin' to say to the police, the Board of Health or nobody else! I want that place closed, I want the grant, and I want it *now!*"

Randall's threatening voice was the last sound for several seconds. Karen simmered in the man's arrogance. She tried to have compassion for the father of an ailing child. He was hurting. She realized that. But he was also disrespectful. Karen's strange silence was intimidating.

"Mr. Harvey," she said, digging her nails into the cushioned armrest of her chair. She heard a sharp crack and looked down to see a chipped nail. *Remain in control,* she thought to herself. "You're obviously upset right now, and that's understandable. Perhaps it would be best if you had some time to think. Make an appointment with my receptionist, and we can talk some other time." She moved to pick up her phone.

"But what you gon' do about…"

"Mr. Harvey!" she yelled with a controlled burst. She collected herself, took a breath, and continued. "I suggest—" She paused. Inhaled and exhaled deeply. "I *strongly* suggest that you take some time to think. Make an *appointment,*" she emphasized. "And maybe we can talk about this some other time. Now, if you'll excuse me—and you *will* excuse me—I need to make a phone call."

Randall glanced at the woman as she returned to her work activities. He headed towards the door and flung it open.

"Mr. Harvey," she said, stopping his exit. "This office is my sanctuary and you will treat it as such. Don't ever storm in here like I work for you or owe you something." The two began a staredown, each daring the other to talk or look away. Karen finally offered a symbolic truce. "I hope your son recovers. I'll be praying for him."

Randall turned and left the office, miffed and confused. Not certain if he'd been insulted or inspired. The receptionist gave him a look of disdain as he walked to the elevator, her last attempt in their personal duel.

Once inside the elevator, Randall pushed the button marked G and waited for the first jerk of the box with sliding doors and unseen gadgets transporting people up and down. He glanced up and saw an elevator inspector's business card overlapping the inspection certificate. The name Lila Mae Watson was above the initials LMW. Randall half wondered if she'd eaten at La Familia, or if she'd ever been to Fish Nets. He wondered which of the two restaurants Karen preferred. The inspection was a validation that the elevator was good, very much like the scores posted in restaurants. The thought of perfect one hundreds plagued him. The highest score his restaurant had ever received was a ninety-five. The lowest was an eighty-one, which by most standards was unsanitary. If an inspector dropped by at the wrong time — even at the wrong second — the result could be disastrous.

On a day when the weekly food delivery had arrived late, a health inspector peered her prying head through the back door. The truck, which normally arrived at ten in the morning, showed up at high noon when there weren't enough people both to unload and take care of the lunch crowd. Randall tried going back and forth from the register to the truck. Forgetting the cardinal rule of food sanitation, he unloaded several boxes, placed them on the floor, and — in a mad rush to retrieve lettuce, tomatoes, and onions — left the boxes uncovered and exposed. The restaurant received deduction points for each uncovered box and each box that had been set down on the floor, even for just a few seconds.

It was that particular incident which caused Randall to marvel at how clean La Familia must have been in order to receive all those perfect scores. He looked at the elevator inspection certificate again and wondered what would happen if a bolt was out of place or the door didn't open fast enough. Would Lila Mae Watson, whoever she was, give the elevator an eighty-one?

His cell phone rang and he pulled it from the belt clip on his pants. It was a new Motorola Randall's oldest son had given him. The only perk of having a failing cell phone business. After fumbling to enable the talk command, he finally caught the caller on the last ring.

"Hello," Randall said, hoping the caller hadn't hung up.

"Hello, Mr. Harvey?"

"Yes."

"Mr. Harvey, it's Dr. Powell over at DeKalb Medical."

"Hey, Doc! Did Jessie come out of his coma?" Randall asked with hopeful excitement.

"No sir. I'm afraid not. But I would like you to come back to the hospital immediately. We've received the test results. It seems that Jessie was poisoned."

"We already knew that, Doc, so what's the big…"

"It's a bit more complicated than that. Your son's nervous system has been severely affected and we're also concerned about respiratory failure. Please come as soon as you can. What we found was something quite…"

Randall was stunned. On autopilot, he was about to click off when he vaguely realized the doctor was still talking. He brought the phone back up to his ear.

"…poison that Jessie and the others ingested. It's very bizarre. Mr. Harvey, the traces of poison we discovered in your son and all the other patients…. Well…to be honest…it can't be found in restaurants."

Chapter Seven
Ugly Beauty

After a mere six hours, Karen Batch managed to eject herself from what was usually a twelve-hour work day. Dealing with the police and with Randall, prompted a much-needed getaway. She decided to take the rest of the afternoon off and get her hair and nails done. It was a good day for some pampering anyway since she and her husband Ethan were having dinner together.

The guilt of leaving work early often sent her back to the office or put her at work extra early the next morning. Today, nothing could make her retreat. She and Ethan rarely were able to spend quality time together. His construction company and Karen's consulting business left little time for leisure events. Their exchange of daily affection was limited to short emails: *I love you, thinking of you, hope your day is going well.*

Tonight, they'd both agreed to make every necessary arrangement in order to have a nice dinner together and then possibly catch a show at the Fox Theater.

The Bayou Cajun Restaurant was their favorite. It was a welcome fine dining addition to a busy street littered with fast food joints and check-cashing stands. The restaurant was never as busy as it should have been, but it was a much needed site for the Black community. It was also just a few miles from the hair salon. She'd arrive at dinner punctual and pretty for her loving husband.

When Karen arrived at the salon, the receptionist was deeply engrossed in a magazine. She glanced up briefly at Karen, then turned the page and resumed her reading.

"Excuse me," Karen said politely.

The girl held up her index finger extended by a long purple nail with pink polka dots. The color scheme matched the Technicolor braids woven into her already twice-dyed two shades of black hair. The young girl's follicles were screaming at Karen. The loud colors yelled, 'look at me' and her roots cried out to be what they once were. They longed to be the pure innocence of a neatly braided ponytail on the morning of school picture day. The morning that all children left home with warnings from parents not to get their nice clothes dirty before the class picture was taken. Pictures of the young girl confused her mother now. She wondered how her precious baby had become this ill-mannered person with rainbow roots. A person who would deliberately ignore a paying customer.

"Excuse me," Karen repeated, more firmly this time.

The extended finger lowered and rolling eyes raised, followed by a tone filled with contempt.

"What chu need?" she asked.

"My name is Karen Batch and I have a three o'clock appointment with Bonnie."

"She not heruh."

"I'm sorry, what did you say? She's not here?"

"That's what I said, she not heruh." the girl said, slightly raising her voice and brutalizing the English language.

A cosmetologist had seen the polka-dot finger raised and heard the beginnings of a potential confrontation. She hurried over before Karen had a chance to respond.

"Hi," she said, politely. "I'm Donna. Are you here to see Bonnie?"

"Yes, I am," Karen replied, baffled that a human acted the way the young girl had. Even more baffled that this human had found and was maintaining a job dealing with people.

"I think she's running a bit late. She had to pick up some beauty supplies from the warehouse."

"Did she call and say she'd be running late?" asked Karen.

"Nawh she 'idn't call. These peoples right heruh waitin' on huh too," the young girl announced, pointing at two other women sitting in chairs, their faces covered by magazines.

Karen glanced at the waiting patrons and back at Donna, who seemed to be in charge of damage control for the salon. The kind cosmetologist looked at Karen with embarrassment and said, "I apologize. She should be here any..."

"Whew, I am sorry I'm late everybody!" Bonnie announced, bursting through the door. "I got behind this eighteen-wheeler that didn't know where he was goin'. Seem like it was gonna stay in front of me forever and then it pulled across the street." The woman was babbling and walking while sliding into her smock preparing for all three customers. "At the last minute the truck pulled into that parking lot across the street and parked in front of that abandoned grocery store. You know I *had* to go see what was goin' on 'cause we need another grocery store over here, bad. Who's first?" she asked, as the whirlwind finally settled to serve her inconvenienced customers.

"These two ladies right heruh was ahead of this lady right heruh. They all want perms. But I 'on't know what this lady wont. She was about to get mad 'cause you late," said the braid-slinging rainbow warrior. Karen was shocked, then offended. It was this type of blatant disrespect for patrons that fueled her passion as a business consultant.

Bonnie hurried to the front again after clearing out three chairs underneath sinks for washing hair. "Y'all have to excuse my cousin," she said. "She left her home-training at home today."

As the women folded their magazines and gathered their purses, they all laughed at Bonnie's comment, except Karen. She was furious and wanted to leave right then, as a personal protest against how they treated customers. But it was already a quarter past three and there was no way she'd find a walk-in salon that could get her manicured and out by dinner. Still, it frustrated her to no end that business was conducted this way in her neighborhood and it didn't seem to affect anyone else in the salon.

Once the women were seated and the prickly droplets of warm water danced through their strands, all was well. Bonnie began washing the first of three ladies and signaled for Karen to have a seat next to the other two. The cosmetologist was skilled and fast. Once the first woman's hair was soaked, she announced, "Let that warm water titillate those roots for a minute, girl." Then she dashed to the next woman and let warm water seep into her hair for a few moments. By that time, Karen was settled and in her seat. "There we go, honey," said Bonnie to the second woman. "Let that head drown in some wet sunshine. Don't it feel good?"

Finally, she danced over to the last chair where Karen was sitting and began soaking her hair, achieving the objective. All three customers—even though they had been overbooked—were given attention and suffused with the anticipation of being beautiful. They were also trapped for the next three or four hours.

The radio pushed mid-afternoon tunes through the speakers, interrupted by hectic traffic updates and occasional weather reports. Bonnie, still bopping from one customer to the next, made conversation with all three women while trying to squeeze in two more customers who were weekly regulars and big tippers.

It was again Karen's turn in the round-robin conversation.

"So how's work goin', lady?" Bonnie asked.

"It's fine. Hectic as usual. Staying busy. How are things here? I see you're staying busy yourself." *Too busy*, she thought.

"Not busy enough, evidently," replied Bonnie. "I had a not-so-pleasant conversation with this old Ching Chong lady at the beauty supply warehouse. You know they tryin' to run us outta business, don't cha?"

"How do you mean?"

"They got these big stores all over our community and sellin' *our* products. And sellin' 'em cheaper than us. Oh, I forgot to ask, I'm just ramblin'. Did you wanna get your nails done? Let me get my cousin over here and get started while you under the dryer. Kikinatreeka! I need you over here for a manicure."

"No, no, no. That's okay. Let Kumbaya CocoPuffs, or whatever her name is, stay right where she is. I need to check out a small business over in that strip mall, so unfortunately that's where I'm getting my manicure today."

Bonnie looked at Karen with a sly smile and joked, "See, you ain't right. Goin' to the competition. Who is it, Nikki's Nails?"

"No, I went there about six months ago and didn't like it. I'm gonna check out Black Beauty."

Bonnie stopped in mid-stride on her way to continue her musical chairs mingling. She turned and spoke, spitting attitude.

"Black Beauty!"

"Yes it's over by..."

"Oh, I know where it is. You gon' let the Ching Chongs do yo' nails 'cause my salon ain't good enough?"

Donna's ears perked up, as did her damage control radar.

Karen—offended by the racial overtone and accusation—said, "No, I'm going because they have faster service and their prices are better. That's simply competitive business. And when I walk in the door, no one throws their polka-dot fingers in my face because they're preoccupied with the latest hair holocaust in a beauty magazine. Which is why they're being considered for a million-dollar grant, along with other successful businesses in the community."

"See, that's what I'm talkin' about. Some of y'all don't know how to recycle the Black dollar and—"

"Uh, excuse me, Bonnie. Not only do I recycle the Black dollar, but I'm recycling fifty-five of them right now. Despite the fact that you were late *and* overbooked. So if you don't mind, I'd rather you not lecture me on the Black dollar, economics, or anything whatsoever that has to do with customer service."

"And what's gon' happen when ain't no mo' Black hair care stores 'cause y'all done bought from the *competitive* store? I met the heifer that owns Black Beauty. Did you know that she buy all the beauty supplies for every Ching Chong around here. And they probably discriminating against Blacks, 'cause the prices she get are way less than the prices I get. Don't you think we need to help each other?" Bonnie said with sass.

"You need to help yourselves. What you call discriminating, they call collective buying power. The more you buy from the distributor, the lower your prices are. Why can't the Black-owned beauty shops get together and buy more products as a group? Why can't three or four shops merge into one, creating a centralized salon and beauty store? I mean, do we really need four different salons on one block? If you consolidated shops, don't you think that would give you more nail technicians in one store and people could get their nails done faster? And by doing so, you get more customers. More satisfied customers, I might add."

"No, we wouldn't get more customers. It's always gon' be people like you that wanna save money and go to the Ching Chongs who use bad quality products. When people keep usin' that stuff, it don't matter how fast we can get you manicured."

"Well, look at your competitors' success. If customers don't mind low-tier products, then it must not be one of their major concerns. Those businesses have realized that, and have passed those cost reductions on to their consumers. As a result, they have a larger market share, which translates into more customers, more business, and more money. And you know, I bet they prefer to be called Asians instead of 'Ching Chong' —just like you would rather not be called jigaboo cosmetologist," Karen added. Her frustration was mounting.

"Girl, I oughta…"

"Did y'all see Judge Mathis yesterday?" Donna blurted. She clutched her hot curlers like a baton-wielding referee declaring a draw in a sporting match.

Bonnie was so into her attack, the interruption startled her. It spooked her just enough to realize that Karen was still a patron. The tingling of blood racing to her head slowed, as did the jumping heart rate.

"Hmmph," Bonnie said as she walked away from Karen and over to the next contestant on *The Overbooked Beauty Salon.*

Karen shook her head and covered her face with an issue of *Black Enterprise*. She laughed after opening the magazine to an article entitled *What Your Business Needs*.

Donna, having stopped the showdown, walked back to her only two customers, but was interrupted by a boisterous woman yelling before the door had been pushed completely open.

"Chile, you not gon' believe what they buildin' across the street! Remember how we said they should put a grocery store there? It's ten times worse. Look at these advertisin' fliers they passin' out."

The women all extended their hands, reaching for the colorful pieces of paper. Each woman read the information, which had been professionally designed and printed. The colors were attractive and the graphics were bold, as was the text. The entire salon fell silent while they examined the fliers. Karen realized the day she had predicted was coming much sooner than she had anticipated. She flipped the flier over and saw that the same message was written on the back in Spanish and Korean.

Bonnie pranced back over to Karen, waving the flier, and said, "You happy now?"

Karen, still deciphering what the flier meant to the community, sat quietly wondering how things had come to this.

Chapter Eight

Philosophers & Traitors

Juan Santos pushed the video into the VCR and mashed the play button of the remote control. He pointed the infrared light further towards the box thinking it might produce a stronger signal—yet he himself was weakened by what was playing out before him.

That Tuesday night, members of his family had gathered to discover who the villain might be. Juan demanded they all leave and allow him to be the only one to view the tape at first. He would find the monster and deliver the punishment himself, if necessary.

The curious man played scenarios in his mind. Perhaps it was a band of misguided youth who knew not the enormity of their deeds. Youth who certainly needed no public prosecution or harsh penalties from what Juan considered a brutal system of justice. Maybe he'd been burglarized by transient men in search of the nourishment they needed to survive one more day. They often stopped by in search of odd jobs, hoping for payment by way of chicken quesadillas. The men needed opportunities instead of sentences, he thought.

Juan sat watching as the electronic snow danced across the screen, distorting the picture. He wondered what he would say to the culprit, if caught on tape, if he ever saw him—or her—in person. Once again he smashed buttons on the remote, trying to adjust the tracking. His arm extended towards the tube, aiming the remote like an invisible laser. The distortion eventually faded to thin horizontal lines and then disappeared completely, leaving nothing but a sharp image of the truth.

Juan's mouth fell open in shock. His hand went limp, dropping the remote onto the hard concrete floor. It fell on its edge and shattered, in much the same way as Juan's trust and forgiving spirit had just been broken. He recognized one of the men in the video. The picture froze when the remote hit the ground. The perpetrators had unknowingly looked into the camera during the escape. Their faces burned deceitful eyes upon Juan.

The second face was not immediately distinguishable. Once the disbelief turned to acceptance, Juan was able to digest the full extent of the betrayal. Anger transformed him into a whirlwind of rage. He stood and slowly walked behind his chair, pondering why this had happened and what he would do. He wondered if he had somehow provoked this action and what would happen if he were to carry out the fatal vengeance swarming his mind.

Juan ripped his fingers into the back of the chair and tossed it towards whatever object had the misfortune of being in its way—a bookshelf holding volumes of Spanish to English and English to Spanish dictionaries, and several volumes of a series entitled *How To Learn English*. The bookcase wobbled unsteadily, then fell over, just as the wooden shelf's ancestor had done in a forest somewhere by some unnatural violent force very much like the violence pumping through Juan's veins. He noticed one of the titles. *English Means Opportunity*. He smiled ruefully, remembering how optimistic and naïve he'd been not so long ago. He kicked the book, launching it into the air. It smashed into a delicate glass clock—a family heirloom of his wife's—that would never keep time again.

People ran into the room when they heard the commotion of the falling bookshelves and the breaking glass. Juan stopped them at the door, yelling, "Salida!"

They looked around the room and saw the destruction, but quickly left. If Juan was speaking Spanish, breaking his own fundamental English-only

72

rule, then his anger was too great to be contained by anyone other than himself or God.

Randall arrived back at the hospital to learn that his son's condition had not improved, nor had it worsened. Visitations were limited to once every four hours, for ten minutes in groups of three. Prior to learning the type of infection, people were required to wear gowns, masks, and gloves in order to protect themselves from what doctors at first believed was an airborne virus. Indeed it was not. The life-squeezing sensation invading Jessie's body was attacking his spinal cord and suffocating his brain. Bypassing the friends and family crowding the waiting room, Randall headed for his son's bedside in the critical care unit. There he found Veronica, Corey, and the doctor who'd called while he was on the elevator.

"How he doin'?" Randall asked.

"Same," replied Veronica.

Randall looked at his son as he lay in bed with tubes trespassing in his mouth. His body was rigid. His hands and feet were extended and stretched as though he'd been electrocuted then frozen an instant later.

Corey stood over the bed, eyes glued to his brother as if he were trying to will him out of the coma.

"Did you talk to that lady, Daddy? She gon' take them Mexicans off the grant list?"

"Naw, babygirl. She think this was some kinda foul play or somethin'. Say that restaurant got the cleanest bill of health in the county, just about."

"Clean!" Veronica exclaimed. "How the hell it's so clean and my baby brother layin' here half dead from eatin' that nasty food! Let me go talk to that bit—"

"Mr. Harvey," the doctor interjected, attempting to restore quiet in the delicate area. "Would you mind if we took a short walk for a moment? Perhaps we'd better let some other visitors see your son for a few moments while we're away." His eyes never left Randall, not wanting the hostile daughter to take offense at his insinuation that she leave. Randall caught on and obliged the doctor's suggestion.

"Veronica, gon' out to the waitin' room and let somebody else come back here to see Jessie. I'm sure the church members want to come back here and pray."

"They can pray from the waitin' room. Why I gotta..."

"Gon' get somebody else to come back here. Don't let me have to ask you again," Randall threatened. Veronica quickly recalled Randall's demeanor from days of old. Days when their patriarch, struggling to play the dual role of mother and father, warned once and spanked twice. Since that time, none of his children stepped across the first warning—not even as adults. The tactic had successfully evolved over the course of their lives. As children they feared him, as teenagers they revered him, and now as adults they respected him.

Veronica rolled her eyes and did as her father asked. He always had problems walking the line between gentle and aggressive with his daughter. It was the mother's touch he could never seem to master.

"Is there a Mrs. Harvey?" asked the doctor.

"Yeah. Somewhere I guess. If she's still alive," Randall replied as the two walked down a hall towards a private consultation room.

"Oh, I'm sorry. Didn't mean to pry."

"Don't worry 'bout it."

"I'm sorry. I feel like an idiot for bringing that up."

"No problem, Doc. We been dealin' wit' it long before now. I just wanna know what's goin' on and when my son is gonna pull through."

The doctor stopped walking and paused in front of a door with a sign that said "Consultations Only." He sighed before answering. Delivering unpleasant news never got easier, only routine. Medical school, his internship, and all his years of practice still left him unprepared for the transformation on family members' faces when they heard the fate of their loved ones. It was especially hard when telling a parent about their child.

"Mr. Harvey, I'm afraid that what Jessie has is more than food poisoning. It was, well, *actual* poison—not something that could have been caused by, say, spoiled chicken or bad beef."

"He ain't got no E. coli or nothin' like that, does he?"

"No, no. It's more serious, actually. We got the toxicology results back rather quickly because we were concerned about the outbreak. And what we've found is a substance called Conium maculatum."

"What?"

"Its more common name is Poison Hemlock."

"What is that?"

"It's actually a plant—similar to a carrot."

"He wasn't eatin' no damn carrots."

"Yes I know, but it has ties to same plant family as carrots. Every part of Poison Hemlock is toxic—some parts more than others. For instance, the root of the plant is more poisonous than the leaves. I know this is of no consolation, but it was the same poison that killed Socrates—the philosopher."

"Back in old times?"

"Yes, that's right."

"That mean y'all must have a cure for it by now, right?"

"Once ingested, it can be treated, yes, but it has to be caught right away. But I'm afraid there is no antidote to speak of. And, Mr. Harvey, in your son's case, it appears that he ingested a very large dose of the poison—perhaps some directly from the root of the plant. It's possible the others got small amounts from the leaves. Poison Hemlock attacks the nervous sys-

76

tem rather aggressively, which is why your son went into convulsions. And to be quite honest, it's a miracle that everyone who was exposed is still alive. We're still trying determine how the poison was used. Whether it was a liquid extraction, or ground particles. This might help us get a better idea of how to fight it."

"But that still sound like that restaurant could have been dirty."

"Well...it's highly unlikely. Poison Hemlock is much more abundant in the western part of the U.S., which further makes us think that it was introduced into the environment by a foreign source."

"What you mean foreign source?"

"As in, it wasn't natural, like bad food. Jessie's been getting a variety of medications for his condition, and now we're waiting to see what happens. It was sort of like getting allergy medicine before you know what you're allergic to. We didn't know what he had so we gave him the best thing we could until we found out."

"I gotcha. So what do we do now? Just wait till he gets better and comes out of it? That can't be no longer than what...couple of days? A week at the most, right?"

"It's not that simple. Your son seemed to get such a large concentration that it was almost like a lightning bolt going through his system. The other victims ingested much less. As a result, none of them had as severe a reaction as your son did. Mr. Harvey, you have to understand that in some cases, Poison Hemlock has been fatal in fifteen minutes."

"And that's why Jessie gon' recover. 'Cause it would'a got him by now, right?"

The doctor paused and sighed once more.

"Jessie's brain has lost a significant amount of oxygen due to the blockage in his brain stem. We performed a CAT scan of his brain and there is a large amount of swelling. I must be honest with you, Mr. Harvey. Jesse has about a twenty-five percent chance of pulling through. And we don't know the full extent of the brain damage he's suffered. Even if he does make it past this critical period, it's likely that he will be a quadriplegic. But I'm more concerned about respiratory failure right now. It seems that is the most common end in cases such as these. I'm very sorry."

Randall stared at the doctor, waiting for his mouth to spew out more hopelessness. He waited, making sure no other sounds would make their way past his lips. Every breath the man made had been torture. Each syllable worse than its predecessor. Randall looked at the doctor, but he saw Jessie, a graduation cap atop his head. The cap fell from his head and Jessie reached down to pick it up and place it back on his crown, but now it was a Little League baseball hat. Randall reached to straighten out his son's cap as he always did before the game. As he reached for the hat, Jessie grabbed his hand and they began a game of mercy. Randall would always let him feel as though he could win and at the last moment bend his wrists backwards with a vein-burning grip. Randall thought he was in that place, in that moment playing with his boy.

"Mr. Harvey...Mr. Harvey" the doctor said, trying to bring the man back from wherever he'd been. "Mr. Harvey, are you all right?"

Randall snapped from his delusion. "Huh? I was...I thought that...Jessie...he."

Randall leaned against the office door to keep from collapsing on the floor. Suddenly, the doctor wished he hadn't brought him this far away from other members of the medical staff in case he needed assistance.

"Mr. Harvey, if you could just step into this office for a moment, I can get you in a seat where you'd be more comfortable."

Randall took the doctor's advice and stumbled through the door. He plunged into the nearest chair and dropped his head into his hands. Immobile for a few moments, he finally raised his head to face reality when he saw two men in conservative suits standing in the corner of the room.

"Mr. Harvey," the doctor began. "These gentlemen are detectives. They want to talk you about your son's poisoning."

Chapter Nine

Memories

Karen entered the Bayou Cajun Restaurant where she found her husband sitting at the bar. A look of frustrated dejection inverted his grin.

"Hey honey," she greeted him. "I'm glad we came to a place like this where somebody has some common sense and knows how to treat customers. You would not believe what happened to me today at the salon."

Noticing that her husband was not his usual attentive self, Karen paused and moved closer to him. Scotch & soda whirled from his breath. Either he'd been there for quite some time or he'd tried to run the place out of scotch before anyone else had a chance to order.

"Are you okay, Ethan?"

"Yeah, baby. I've just got a few things on my mind. Your hair looks nice. Let's go over and have a seat." He always noticed her. New hairstyle, manicured nails, new outfit with matching shoes. He paid careful attention to the details of his wife and she loved him dearly for it.

"How many drinks have you had?" she asked.

"Not enough. I've got some bad news, Karen," he said, dropping into a corner booth.

"Good evening," the server said. He rushed over to greet them and placed menus on the table. "May I start you out with something to drink?"

"Lemonade for me and water for my husband," Karen said, giving Ethan a look. Abashed, he lowered his head and smiled with renewed appreciation of his wife's smothering concern.

"You know, why don't we go ahead and order. I'll have the blackened chicken pasta. Ethan, do you know what you want?"

"I'll have the same," Ethan replied. He'd eaten there so many times the menu was ingrained on his taste buds.

"I'll get that right out," the server replied, hurrying off to the kitchen.

"I love this place," Karen said. "Now what's the bad news? Is that why you were over there swimming in your scotch?"

"I did have a little too much, didn't I? Well, here's the deal. Good news, I'll be home more to finish up the project around the house. Bad news, I was gonna get you a new Jag for Christmas. Worse news, I lost the contract for the project over on Memorial Drive. Remember the big secret that no one knew about? I guess the right people knew about it and the right people knew how much to bid."

"You're kidding. I thought you had the inside track on that project. That was gonna put you in another league of construction, wasn't it?"

"The inside track I had was the outside track compared to this other company. You realize that it was a six-month commitment and all kind of doors would have been opened for me if we'd gotten that job, don't you?"

"Oh Ethan, I'm so sorry. Is there anything I can do? Anyone I can call?"

"No. I doubt it. Grapevine says I was underbid by forty percent! Can you imagine that?"

"Really! Who can make a profit with a contract that low? And will the job be done right?"

"Oh yeah, it'll be done right. And they'll make a profit. These guys are runnin' contractors out of business."

"What guys?"

"Santos Construction."

Karen felt her lungs freeze for a second, just long enough to make her feel a little dizzy.

"Juan Santos?"

"I think that's the owner. You know him?"

"He's being considered for the grant...his restaurant, that is. I had no idea he had a construction company."

"These guys have all these family members they brought over from Mexico. When they get here, before they even become citizens they're replacing windows on a job site. Pouring concrete, landscaping, putting up sheetrock. And working fourteen-hour days. Before they even know it, the immigrants have more experience than guys working five years.

"I had this Hispanic guy on one of my indoor crews trying to work two days because his regular crew was waiting on the weather to pass for an outdoor job. He tells me everything about their operation. They've got three families living in one apartment so the rent is almost nothing. All the families work for Santos Construction and the company buys groceries and helps pay their utilities. As a result, they can pay them a much lower wage, undercut me and anybody else that wants to make a decent profit on a job.

"They get to the site an hour before the job begins and they leave an hour after everybody else is gone. And get this, they throw so many men on a job it gets done in half the time and then they're off to another job. Not only did they underbid me by forty percent, but they beat my schedule by three months. How can I compete with that? How can anybody compete with them? They're gonna own the construction industry ten years from now. You know that, right?"

The words were piercing to Karen. Her attempts to help the community had actually wound up hurting her own household. The Santos workers and other immigrants were far hungrier for opportunities, having never received them in their homelands. They were willing to sacrifice and collaborate. They were doing, she thought with a start, exactly what Juliet Lee was doing at Black Beauty—banding together to gain a competitive advantage.

"So you think Santos Construction is the same guy that owns La Familia?" she asked.

"You mean the Mexican place that poisoned all those people?"

"It may not have been poisoning, but yeah, that's the one."

"I wouldn't doubt it. The guy that worked my crew for two days said they own construction, restaurants, landscape, janitorial services, and God knows what else."

Karen reached in her purse to retrieve the frightful flier she'd been given in the salon.

"Is this the project you bid on?" Karen asked.

Ethan examined the architectural rendering and the address at the bottom of the page. His eyes widened and his lips pressed tightly together.

"This is it! This is the job we were supposed to get and finish in eight months. How in the hell can this be opening so soon if they just won the bid? This must mean that…"

Karen interjected, "They got the contract before the bidding even started."

Juan Santos now walked the earth as he had never done—with contempt for his own people. For the past four days, he'd been watching the video. Wondering how to react, trying to figure out who the second person was. He didn't know whom to trust, whom to banish, and whom to hold close. An unspoken creed had been violated when he watched the video and saw one of his former employees involved with the sabotage. It was a person who had slept under his roof and eaten his food when he arrived from Mexico.

Juan knew about the man's family and their problems in Juarez—a city surviving from the bountiful crumbs of El Paso. The man and his family were professional beggars. By day, the wife would stroll the tourist area. An enlarged stomach tumor made her look pregnant and people gave her money out of sympathy; others gave just to make her move along so they would not have to witness the depressing sight.

By night, the man's 10-year-old son would stand at traffic lights holding a cup of gas and a flaming wooden stick. When the light halted curious drivers, he'd stand in front of the cars and pour the gasoline into his mouth. He'd then project the poisonous liquid towards the stick, creating a fiery fountain for all to see. He hoped they'd reward him with tips for his bravery — or desperation.

The father begged for jobs and seldom got them, so he tried to supplement his rare handouts with pick-pocketing. Juan knew of his misfortune and arranged for the man and his family to cross the border. However, it was now apparent that the suffering had filled the man with greed and malice. A part of him wanted to send the man back to Juarez or have his son perform his fire-spitting act a few inches from the father's face. The other part of him wanted to embrace the man with an unconditional love of family. It was all Juan knew, family. It was why he worked, why he had left his native land, and most of all why he would not turn the man in to the authorities.

The only fiber of redemption came through seeing that the other trespasser in the video was not Hispanic. His anger turned to curiosity as he repeatedly tried to recall where he had seen the other face. Was it one of the many transients he'd hired to sweep the front walk, compensated only by a meal or a coupon for free nourishment? Or was it one of the few people he'd escorted out of the restaurant in haste because of lewd behavior? Proportionally, Juan had made many more friends than enemies. But the small number of enemies had obviously been enough to produce this two-person team of intruders. Though the camera was not able to capture what the men had actually done in the restaurant, it was Juan's belief that they were the people responsible for poisoning his customers, his family, and his community.

With one more close viewing of the tape and a mental checklist of places he'd seen and people he'd met, Juan suddenly matched a face with an event and recognized the second person. With the same rage he'd experience upon his initial viewing of the tape, he stormed about his office once again feeling angry and betrayed. What had he done to warrant this attack? The answer was unclear, although his response would be clear to all. Fuming with vengeance, Juan threw back the doors of his closet and anxiously jiggled keys into a locked box. He grabbed something from the box and jetted out towards his truck. Thinking he might know where to find the second intruder, Juan headed out, trying his best to conceal the .38 caliber tucked into his pants.

Chapter Ten

Mexican Fish Beauty

Sunbeams speared through a filmy layer of smog trying to dampen the morning sky over Memorial Drive. The rush hour cars had already projected their carbons into clouds, adding to the ever-growing problem of a choking atmosphere. In a couple hours, the routine would begin all over again for the lunch breaks. A few people, some of whom had gone to work early, made their way to restaurants of choice ahead of the noontime rush. One of these people, a tall, stylish woman, entered Randall's establishment in hopes of eating in quick solitude. Today was Veronica's turn at the helm of the restaurant while the others attended to Jessie back at the hospital. He still showed no signs of improvement. Veronica stood behind the counter, shouting commands to the back and never making eye contact with the lady standing before her.

"What you gon' have?" Veronica asked.

"Hi, how are you doing?" the woman said, smiling, hoping to get the same in return. Veronica kept completing small tasks. Rolling register tape, organizing to-go containers, pulling wrinkles out of bags — all unnecessary and all designed to avoid eye contact or courtesy. Realizing Veronica was not going to reciprocate the greeting, the woman gave her order.

"I'll have a seafood salad and bottled water, please. Could you — "

"The salads ain't ready yet."

"Excuse me?"

Veronica looked at the woman, dumfounded. She thought she'd spoken as clearly as possible. She repeated her message, slow and deliberate.

"Salads — ain't — ready — yet."

"Well, how long before they're ready?"

Veronica sighed, then yelled to the back. "How long 'fore them salads ready?"

A man shouted from the kitchen area, unconcerned about any customers within earshot. "The crabmeat ain't thawed out! They ain't take it out this morning when they got here. I got some crabmeat from yesterday, but it might not be good."

"So how long it's gon' be?" Veronica asked.

"'Bout forty-five minutes."

89

"It's gon' be forty-five minutes," Veronica said, turning to the woman as though the yelling from the kitchen hadn't been heard.

"For a salad? Don't you think that's unreasonably long?"

Veronica looked at the woman for the first time, twitched her mouth to one side, and shrugged her shoulders.

Okay, I see this is going to be a good one, the woman thought. "How about a fish sandwich?"

"What kind of fish?"

"What kind do you recommend?"

"Whatever kind you want."

"Is there a type more popular than the others?"

"Catfish."

"Is that filet or whole?"

"How you gon' eat a whole catfish sandwich? You know it got bones in it," Veronica snipped.

The woman stood in disbelief. She was puzzled for a moment, wondering if she was really a customer. Remembering why she was here, she carried out her mission.

"Ma'am, could you please give me a catfish sandwich and a bottle of water to go?"

"Ain't no bottled water. It's in the soda fountain machine."

"You know what, fine. Just the sandwich, please, so I can get out of here and…nothing."

Off the woman went, huffing out of the front door. She threw the order into the closest trash receptacle.

Veronica paid no attention and returned to her inconsequential tasks.

After storming out of Randall's place, the woman made her way over to La Familia. Despite the controversy, she'd wanted to go for quite some time. Juan's convincing speech and waving of perfect scores had helped a little, but the lunchtime crowd had not yet returned to its normal size. The long lines outside the door had been reduced to a few devout customers, stragglers passing through, and people who had never heard about the food poisoning.

Once inside, the woman smelled delicious spices dancing through the air and fresh warm tortillas. She decided that whatever she smelled, was what she wanted to order. Before the woman even made it to the menu board, a personable Hispanic woman with dark eyes and a spreading smile called out, "Bievendido! Welcome to La Familia. How are you today? May I recommend the chicken quesadillas?"

Shocked by the enthusiastic greeting, the woman was speechless for a few seconds. She paused. "Sure, why not. I'll take an order to go."

"Ohhh," the order-taker said in jovial disappointment. "You won't be eating in the dining room today? Free refills on your beverage and free chips and salsa if you stay here."

"Okay, well..." The woman was amazed at the overwhelming customer service. "You got it. I'll eat here and if I have room left over, I'll order dessert.

You don't have bottled water by any chance, do you?"

"Of course we do. I'll put in an order for a small chicken quesadillas. That way you'll have more room for dessert. Four twenty seven, please."

As the cashier accepted the woman's five-dollar bill, she smiled and said, "Thank you, ma'am. Please sit anywhere you like. Have a great day." She then turned to another person walking through the door and spoke with the same enthusiasm. "Bievendido! Good to see you again, sir. Welcome to La Familia. How are you? Will you be having the usual?"

The woman walked towards the condiment table to get napkins and utensils. She was stopped by the cashier.

"Ma'am!"

"Yes?" the woman replied, a bit startled.

"Your order is ready. A small chicken quesadillas and a bottle of water. Enjoy your meal."

"Whoa. That was fast."

The cashier just smiled and turned to the next customer, whom she greeted warmly She gave the rehearsed and courteous phrase.

On the way to a cozy, clean booth, with tray in hand, the woman laughed at the differences between La Familia and Fish Nets. She'd had already forgotten the name and soon, she thought, so would everyone else.

There was one more stop the woman had to make before darting back to her office, where pounds of paperwork and mountains of messages awaited her return. The last errand was Black Beauty, where the products were so plentiful, inventory control could be nothing short of wishful thinking.

At the register was a gentle old Asian woman and a younger woman who appeared to be her daughter. Pictures of beautiful Black women with trendy hairstyles were plastered on the walls. Everywhere the woman turned, a model made over to perfection stared back at her. Shelves were covered with different styles of brushes and combs in multiple colors. Hair gel, oils, and shampoos fought for space only to be quickly replenished by more cases, day after day. Customers ran in every day after work, grabbing a plethora of products at bargain prices.

There were hot curlers that weren't even seen in most beauty salons; elaborate hair dryers and compact models that could fit into a small purse; manicure and pedicure tools stretching all the way down to the back wall. If something promised or even suggested the possibility of beauty, it could be found here.

The woman walked passed the Asian ladies and smiled. They returned the gesture, but looked at her cautiously. "If there anyteeng you need, we help you no problem."

"Okay. Thank you." Off she walked towards the back of the store. The woman wanted everything she saw, but needed none of it. Then she remembered that a co-worker had asked her to pick up a hair wrap if she saw one. The woman didn't have time to look, so she turned to walk back to the front and ask the ladies. To her surprise, one of the women was standing a few feet behind her and the other was directly across from her on the next row.

"Do you have any hair wraps?" she asked puzzled as to why the woman was standing so close to her.

The younger replied with rapid-fire speech, "Hair wrap aisle three, middle section, second shelf, left side, next to scarf and shower cap."

"Well…thank you." *They really know their products. Very impressive*, the woman thought to herself.

After she'd located the hair wrap in exactly the spot the woman described, the woman saw a basket of loofah sponges near the front of the same aisle. She walked towards them, thinking that hers was a bit worn out. Always a careful shopper, she remembered the price of loofah sponges at Wal-Mart, but couldn't compare the price here because it wasn't shown anywhere. She decided to ask. As she turned around, she nearly tripped over the older woman. The younger woman had maneuvered her way to the front of the aisle.

"How much are these loofah sponges?" she asked, slightly annoyed.

The human price scanner replied again, "Loofah sponges two ninety nine. Three for five dolla."

"Thank you," she said, walking away from the women. This time she went to a remote corner of the store where no one would happen to be if she weren't being followed. Without warning, she quickly turned around. Sure enough, there they were once again, four feet away and one aisle over.

She'd had enough cat and mouse. She charged up to the register, placed the items on the counter, and waited for the woman to ring her up. As soon as the first button was touched the woman spoke, "I think I've changed my mind. You can put all of this back on whatever aisles on whatever shelf in whichever section, right next to whatever else. If I wanted to walk around the store with other women I would've brought my girlfriends."

In a blast of frustration, the woman jumped in her car and sped back to work. All the while, she made mental notes of each business, thinking what she would say about them in her official mystery shopper report.

Chapter Eleven

Vengeance is No One's

The A-list of supporters was getting shorter each day. What was once a waiting room filled with extended family, friends, neighbors, and folks coming to simply pray, had dwindled down to immediate family and a few folks who still wanted to pray. A week had passed and Jessie hadn't moved.

Hospital staff had called Randall during the night and asked that he return to the hospital and gather the family. Jessie's condition had worsened and his prognosis was dismal. The praying folks began their own vigils throughout the waiting room. Walking and praying, they took on the appearance of angels or ghosts moving amongst the living. When the spirit hit, a praying person would touch a part of the hospital, a door, a wall, or a piece of equipment, summoning healing powers from wherever they might be lurking. One of the praying persons bunkered down in the chapel, speaking in tongues. The powerful language danced across her lips like a curling wind chime fighting then dancing with sudden gusts. The sounds flew from her mouth, speeding and swirling through the air as though God's war cry was being trumpeted through human vocal chords and only those that recognized the power of such deity could understand the strategic plans for this battle.

She shouted the sounds against the walls and let them bounce from corner to corner until the room was filled with Holy Ghost power. Her hands extended towards the ceiling, though in her mind there was no ceiling here. She awaited what would be sent down. Healing powers within her hands, visions of how to cure the sick, answers to why this had happened, or whatever God's will would be.

A visitor who hadn't been to the hospital since the incident walked by the chapel. He was all too familiar with the sound of women crying out for their families, waiting for miracles to drop down from the sky and fully having the faith that it would happen just in time.

He kept walking and entered the waiting room, where faces darker than his greeted him with malicious eyes.

97

"Daddy, ain't that—" Corey said to his father.

Randall jumped from his seat and stepped on people's toes, leaping over furniture to rush at Juan Santos.

Juan shot an evil glance at Corey, daring him to follow his father.

"What chu think you doin' here? We don't want nothin' you got to say!"

"You owe someting to my family!" Juan exclaimed, not backing down a bit from Randall.

"Uh, I don't know where y'all think y'all at, but it ain't here," a wide-body nurse said, rising from her desk. "Both of you need to get some sense and get outside."

The two marched out like opponents entering an arena. Never taking their eyes off one another, they finally stopped by the side of the building.

"How you gon' come up my face talkin' about I owe you somethin'! My son is layin' in critical care from eatin' at yo' place and I owe you somethin'!"

"Why you try to close my restaurant and destroy my family?"

"Fool, what are you talkin' about?"

"You try to make my business look bad. I know, I hab tape. You send someone to my restaurant to hurt my business. I hab seen."

"What the hell are you..."

They were interrupted by one of the prayer warriors touching the side of the building. Randall recognized him from the church. It was a thin man covered with thinning hair. A thick mustache, a peppered beard. He'd begun making laps around the perimeter of the hospital, praying and asking, praying and listening. He, too, had begun to speak in tongues, begging for healing, hoping for the miracle. Not once did he break stride until he turned the corner. With his eyes closed, mouth open, and hand reaching, the man looked as though an invisible boulder had plummeted from the heavens and landed on earth, crushing his spirit.

Randall heard him mumbling, "Yes, God. If that is your will." The man, who had been praying with unrelenting power, sat on the ground and wept.

Randall and Juan looked on, their dispute momentarily on hold. Juan wondered what the man was doing. Randall tried to rub away the tingling feeling in his chest. His stomach was queasy. It was a discerning feeling of doom. It was the feeling of death.

"Daddy! Daddy!" Veronica screamed, running around the corner. "He gone, Daddy! My baby brother is gone!" Corey ran around the corner, following Veronica. His eyes were swollen with tears. Sweat beaded on his skin, ran down his cheek, and saturated his neck. Suddenly, he charged at Juan. His thundering fist smashed Juan's jaw and knocked him to the ground. Corey started the gangster beatdown routine and kicked Juan in his ribs, head, and back.

Veronica joined her brother in an angry frenzy. She kicked Juan again and again as he rolled into a fetal position, trying to protect his vital areas.

"You killed my little brother!" Veronica screamed. "You killed him!" she repeated, screaming and kicking.

"Don't you ever come around us no mo'! You hear me!" Corey shouted, almost out of breath from emotion and exertion.

Juan could taste blood filling his mouth. He knew that a well-placed blow could have been his demise. He rolled away from his torturers, reached in his pants, and drew the gun he'd stashed away. He pointed it at Corey's head, then at Veronica and back at Corey. He shifted his aim back and forth towards whoever was closest.

"Don't do this! I done lost one already! Corey, Veronica, y'all get away! Come from over there!" Randall shouted when they didn't move fast enough. When they were in reach, he grabbed his children and pushed them behind him, as though fatherhood had transformed him into an invincible human shield.

The praying man had risen to his feet and was quietly chanting, "The blood of Jesus, the blood of Jesus…"

Juan waved the gun around, wanting to kill them for beating him so badly. He was bleeding from a cut in his forehead where Veronica had landed a heel kick and felt burgeoning bruises all over his body. He collected himself as he slowly, painfully got up from the ground, pointing the gun at Randall.

Juan looked at a spot between Randall's eyes, just above his nose. He said, panting, still barely holding

on to his own life, "You have brought this on yourself."

Chapter Twelve

Interrogation

Detective Chris Askew, a thin, Black man two days from his last shave, was talking to Veronica and Corey trying to get as much information as possible. Corey refused to talk to him, didn't even want to say Jessie's name. Veronica was of no help. In between crying and outbursts, more crying and more outbursts, she had nothing to offer.

"I don't think they gonna be much help. They just too upset. Why don't y'all go on home," Randall said, entering the room with two cups of water. After the poison outbreak, Randall figured that he was sure to get the grant and had been getting bids on a remodeling project for the restaurant. Randall had planned to close the restaurant for renovations a few weeks after the announcement was made about the grant recipient. Now, a few days after the funeral, this seemed like a much better time. Randall temporarily closed the restaurant shortly after Jessie's funeral in order to let his children grieve.

He knew Veronica and Corey would not be able to work in the building for quite a while. Randall decided he would take the lowest bid for the project and use some of the grant money to live on until the restaurant reopened.

"Thank you," said the detective, taking the cup and sucking through the straw. "Mr. Harvey, your children can't seem to recall any confrontations that your business may have had. Maybe an upset customer?"

"Detective, I don't mean to be rude, but I want you to find who did this. I mean I want you to find 'em bad. Forgive me if this sounds disrespectful 'cause I'm not myself right now. But why the hell you askin' me these questions? Ain't you supposed the be askin' that Mexican place this stuff? I ain't had no poison food at my place."

"Yessir, that's true. It's my job to follow all leads, uncover every stone, you know."

"Yeah, that's all fine and well. Seem like you'd be talkin' to them dirty wetbacks. That's all I'm sayin'."

Just as Randall landed the racial slur, the detective swallowed a sip of water and coughed as it ran down his windpipe. His eyes watered and closed as violent coughs interrupted the conversation. "You all right, detective?"

"Fine, yes, I'm fine," he managed to say, holding his hand in the air and releasing the last of his throat wrestling. "Was there any bad blood between you and Mr. Santos?" He coughed one last time.

"Huh?" Randall asked, surprised by the question.

"You two were in competition—you served different kinds of food, but you were still competitors, weren't you?"

"Yeah. And?"

"Well, I was just curious to know if there have been any altercations, arguments, or anything of that nature between the two of you."

"Hell nawh. I don't talk to him and he bedda not talk to me. Especially now. What I want to talk to him about? Ain't got nothin' to say. Matter fact, I ain't got nothin' else to say to you either. Over here interrogatin' me. Like I told you before, you need to be talkin' to them Mexicans!" Randall walked over to the detective and grabbed the cup from his hand. He'd extended enough hospitality, more than was required, he felt, during a trying and tragic time such as this.

"If you need somethin' else from me or my family, you call first and ask me what you need to know over the phone. I ain't got time for this kinda foolishness. Don't know who taught you how to be a detective, but they ain't do a very good job. The door is that way," Randall said, pointing towards the front and walking away from the detective.

"Mr. Harvey, I was trained at the police academy just like all of the other officers who protect your home and business. In the future, if I have questions, I'll stop by whenever I want and ask whatever I want. If you don't like it, you can meet me at the station, or I can come pick you up and give you a ride in the back of my car. I'm sorry for your loss and you have my condolences. But you gotta realize, this isn't just about sabotage or food poisoning anymore, Mr. Harvey. It's a homicide."

Chapter Thirteen

Why the Chicken Crossed the Menu

"They followed you around the store?"

"Can you believe that? If I hadn't been mystery shopping, we would have been fighting up in there."

Several days had passed since Karen's mystery shopper had made her rounds. They were to meet at Karen's office and discuss the evaluations, but after a brief conversation on their cell phones, Karen knew there would be no need for deliberation.

"Listen, I don't think we'll be able to meet this afternoon. From the sound of things, we don't need to. I guess Santos is gonna get the grant."

"Karen, there couldn't be a more deserving business. Their quality was great and customer service was unbelievable. I'm beginning to think myself that they were set up for that food poisoning. What have the other mystery shoppers found in their visits?"

"Pretty much been the same as what you've just mentioned. I'm sorry to hear about your experience at Black Beauty. It's really unfortunate, because I'd heard so many good things about Ms. Lee's distribution and the inventory control. I was hoping that small businesses could learn from a great example of globalization like hers."

"Now, don't get me wrong. Their inventory was amazing and I can only attribute the great prices to finding the best suppliers, but the final test is how you treat the consumer. For all that great business infrastructure, they took twenty steps backwards."

"That's sad. Well, thanks anyway. You all have done a great job. Oh, what about Randall Harvey's place? Any luck?"

"Please. Are you kiddin' me? I don't know how they made it this far."

"Great food is how they made it this far."

"Karen, I wouldn't know. They made me so mad I didn't even eat it. Why Black folks think that a cash register and a hours of operation sign are the only things you need to have a successful business?"

Karen laughed out loud, amused by her associate, but concealed her true concerns.

"When I get home I'll e-mail you all of the results, okay?"

There was a silence. Karen was pondering.

"You know something, I don't think that would be enough," Karen said. Her tone was thoughtful.

"You need more than that? I thought it was clear cut."

"The decision is clear cut, yes. But I don't think visiting the stores and evaluating them is enough. Not if we really want to empower the community. Which is what we started out to do, right?"

"Yeah, that was our mission. We can only help businesses that want to help themselves."

"Exactly, but we have to make an effort to help them, even if it's not with a million-dollar grant."

"Okay, so what do we do?"

"How about this? Instead of writing an evaluation, draft a letter for me to send out to the businesses that won't get the grant. Detail all the things you noticed that hurt their success. Get the input of the other mystery shoppers also. Almost make it a scare tactic. Let them know that their business is in jeopardy if they don't pay attention to the shortcomings we've noticed. Make it lengthy, clear, and brutally honest. Can you do that for me?"

"Sure. I love it. I'm pulling up to my office right now and I'll get right on it. You wanna stop by later and take a look at it?"

"No, just e-mail it to me. I'm down near the airport in Hapeville. Gonna pick up a chicken sandwich at McDonald's and call it a day. I'll read it in the morning. Take care."

"Talk to ya soon."

Karen pressed the end button on her phone just as she arrived at the menu board of a McDonald's drive thru. Someone had been having spit target practice at the Big Mac picture. Time-hardened chewing gum stuck to the display, mingled with the saliva residue. The assorted colors of gum that had missed the burger target were stuck to the order screen, the asphalt, and the shoddy attempts at landscaping. Her appetite was momentarily gone, but the hunger was too intense to drive away.

After Karen had been sitting at the intercom box for a full minute and a half, a voice blared through the perforated screen, each hole projecting static. The voice was preceded by laughter. In some language indigenous to those who just don't give a damn about anything other than being ghetto fabulous, an order taker sang with an awkward rhythm, "My name is Keeee—sha. I'm from Eeeast Pernt. Can I take yo' orrrrduh?"

"Excuse me?" Karen asked, unsure if she should simply drive off.

The voice returned after more laughter. This time there was no rhythm and no singing, simply a rushed and rude, "What chu want?"

Karen looked at the intercom box in disbelief. There could not possibly have been a human being attached to a headset making grunts at customers like the one she'd just heard. It wasn't possible. She waited for another grunt but heard nothing.

"Uh, I *think* I'd like a grilled chicken sandwich and a water," she said cautiously.

"A cup or a balluh," the voice cackled.

"A cup or a what?" Karen asked.

"A cup o' wada or a balluh o' wada."

"Uh, a bot-tle of water would be nice," Karen over-articulated in hopes that the voice would do the same.

Her effort was met with silence then a boisterous, "Grilled chicken sammich, balluh o' wada fo' eighty fo' drive to da furce winda."

With one foot on the brake and gear shift in hand, Karen placed the car in reverse, preparing to jet out of the parking lot. Hunger pains were being surpassed by the headache pains spiraling up from her neck and pulsating around her temples. She could only imagine what was attached to the headset shouting ear pollution in the form of broken, beaten down, mangled, pulverized, and regurgitated English.

Her rearview mirror was suddenly filled with bright bursts of headlights pulling up behind her, waiting for their turn to get yelled at and misunderstood by the voice. There was also a car in front of her. She was trapped and would soon be caught in the wrath of whatever lurked in the hellish depths of window number one.

The car in front of Karen played thunder-battling hip-hop sounds that rattled its own trunk. The bass was so invasive, fillings were being loosened in Karen's teeth. She could see only the crowns of the passengers' heads. The rest of their bodies were swallowed by the bucket seats of their restored 1980s car. It was now in vogue to ride partially in the front and partially in back. Seeing over the dashboard for the purpose of avoiding oncoming traffic was completely secondary.

Karen remained there, trapped, massaging her temples and locking her jaws. Finally, the bass invaders pulled ahead to window number two. One car closer to the voice and one window away from freedom. Exhaust fumes clouded the area ahead of Karen's car, prompting her to remain in her space until the blue smoke dissipated. *Thousands of dollars on a sound system, but they won't spend twenty-five dollars on an oil change*, she thought. As the cloud lessened, Karen fixed herself to pull up.

Before she pressed the accelerator, a head sprang from window number one. It looked out on both sides of the drive-thru window and rared back inside. Suddenly the head, with body attached, shot through the window, giving extra force, distance, and velocity to the gigantically despicable wad of spit the person hurled out into the parking lot. Karen was aghast. This hadn't just happened. There was no way that someone was flinging body fluids from a drive-thru window in front of customers and being paid at the same time. A high-pitched horn from a foreign car behind Karen jolted her and forced her to finally come face to face with what she thought would be the venom-spitting head. She turned and saw a face that wasn't the spitter's, but just as alarming.

Underneath the headset , or as close as hair would allow, was a monstrosity of tangled, gelled, and braided hair. Finger waves emulating an aborted conk pasted the sides of the employee's head. Above the conk/fingerwave/whatever were corn-rolled braids dangling down, holding on for dear life by the thread of what real follicles were left. As if the head hadn't suffered enough, a long black fake ponytail sprouted from the top of the person's head. The head looked like an abstract sculpture of a gladiator's helmet after being demolished in war.

"Fo' eighty fo'," it said. *This must be Keeee – sha from Eeeeeast Pernt*, thought Karen.

"Excuse me," Karen began. "Is it normal for people to spit out of the drive thru window in front of customers just before they eat?"

"Oooh nawh somebody didn't!" the helmet-headed hairdooed person replied. She was either shocked that someone had done so or elated that there was another story to be laughed at over the headset. "Was it a gurl or a boy?"

"Does it matter? It was someone who works here."

"Um jes sayin'. If it's a boy, I know who done it. He ain't even 'sposed to be back heruh in drive-thru no way. He make me sick. That'll be fo' eighty fo'."

Karen was irritated. Did heavy-head not know or care that a customer had a legitimate concern? She handed her a five-dollar bill, took her change, and pressed on one window closer to the promised land of the parking lot's exit sign.

"Chicken salad sandwich and walluh?" the occupant of the next window asked. His uniform was falling off his body like someone was yanking it toward the ground. A black doo-rag peeked from underneath his hat, which was cocked to the side in order to give onlookers a better view of his diamond earrings.

"No, I ordered a *grilled* chicken sandwich. If I'm not mistaken, you all don't serve chicken salad sandwiches," said Karen, with boiling frustration.

"Oh. My bad," the window worker said, reexamining the order screen. "That's what I meant. Grilled chicken sandwich."

Without a "thank you," a "get out of my face," or even a "we don't need your stinking money," the worker gave Karen a brown bag presumably containing the proper sandwich and a warmish bottle of water. He closed the window as if she had never been there at all. *Fair enough,* she thought. *I wanted to get away from them just as bad.*

Karen wondered how it had come to be this way. How had customer service been whisked away like a trendy business fad? How were companies surviving with employees like Head-Hell and the Olympic Spitter interacting with customers? She then resigned herself to the notion that people would get what they paid for. McDonald's prices meant McDonald's quality. No, that was no excuse, she thought. Was there a common link to this type of treatment? Did it mean anything that the employees were Black? She thought about the evaluations of her mystery shoppers and realized which business presented the worst customer service: Randall's. The Black business. Was bad service related somehow to Black communities? Too many questions and too many thoughts too late in the day, she decided.

Her car was zooming down the interstate, the soothing sounds of Clark Atlanta's jazz station calming her frazzled nerves. With her deep thoughts leaving her mind as fast as the cars she whipped by, Karen reached in her bag to satisfy her renewed hunger pains. Much to her delight, the order was correct and there was indeed a grilled chicken sandwich awaiting consumption. *This wasn't so bad*, she thought. Perhaps she had been overreacting and maybe a bit judgmental.

She maneuvered her food and steering wheel to finally take a bite of the long-awaited objective. Her teeth pressed through soft, warm bread, crisp lettuce, creamy cool mayonnaise, juicy ripe tomatoes, and the grilled chicken breast. Partly through the sandwich, Karen yanked the steering wheel hard to the right, disregarding any cars that might have been behind her. She just barely caught the last chance at an exit ramp. Quickly hitting the overpass and merging back onto the interstate, Karen darted back to McDonald's to return her chicken sandwich—brown on the outside—completely raw pink and rubbery on the inside.

Chapter Fourteen

Shoot the Messenger

It was Saturday and Fish Nets had been closed for almost two weeks. Randall had managed to deal with the first stages of his grief and give some much-needed attention to remodeling his business. Days flashed by, but the nights tortured along slowly. Randall found a place and time each day for private solitude to release hidden tears for Jessie. He cried for the day he'd unbolted the training wheels from the boy's small bike. He cried for the time he would never witness him walking down the aisle with a beautiful bride in tow. He cried for the day the boy brought home his first picture to be placed proudly on the refrigerator door. He cried for the phone call he would never get announcing his grandson had been named after him. He cried every day for all the days passed and all the days lost.

Normally at this time he would have been gearing up for Saturday's rush. Instead, Randall was going through a stack of bills and deciding who would get paid, who would get partially paid, and who would get ignored until the next billing statement. Corey entered the office with pain running down his face.

"Pops, I need to talk to you."

"What is it, son?" Randall asked without looking up. He ripped open another bill, glanced at the large amount and due date, then discarded it.

"Pops, I need to talk about the business."

"Corey, now ain't the time for another one of your ideas. I thought we was through with that." The next envelope had a big red "Last Notice" stamped on it. Randall put it in his "pay immediately" stack.

"This ain't about a new business. It's about this business. The one I was gonna inherit one day."

"Don't worry son. We gon' get back on our feet real soon. I gotta good feelin' about the grant. Been easin' my way under that lady's...What the hell?"

"What is it, Pops?" Corey asked.

"It's a letter from the grant committee. From Karen Batch." Randall glanced over the long letter and saw the words mystery shopper. "Did y'all get mystery shopped?" he asked, looking at Corey for the first time since he'd entered the office.

"I don't know."

"What chu mean you don't know?"

"If it was a mystery shopper, how would I know?" Corey answered.

Randall, who'd been thinking of ways to prepare for the shopper, realized he'd missed the opportunity. Then he thought of the worst possible scenario: Veronica on the cash register. He'd wanted to have another talk with her, tell his daughter how important it was that she go above and beyond for weeks following his meeting with Karen and the grant finalists. But he never had the talk, putting off another conversation in which Veronica would once again protest that she treated everyone the same. That it was the customers that set her off and if they had better attitudes, she'd treat them better. Now it was too late.

"Pops, can I talk to you right quick?"

"Corey! I ain't got time right now!" Randall exclaimed. He turned his back to Corey and hunched over the letter, pulling at its edges, wishing that the tension on the paper might change the painful words.

LETTER TO BUSINESS OWNERS

Dear Community Business,

Your company has been mystery shopped and the results have been less than favorable. It is with deep regret that we inform you that your company is in trouble. Whether you are a part of a franchise or a sole proprietor, it has been determined that your current business practices are not only detrimental to your future but your community as well.

During a recent visit, a customer visited your facility and received nothing but disrespectful service and/or a mediocre product. It is our attempt to eradicate businesses

such as yours from existence unless you are willing and able to make significant changes in the ways you treat customers.

The easiest solution would be to report you to the Better Business Bureau and inform all potential customers of your deplorable practices. However, we realize it's very easy to criticize rather than enlighten, which we believe every dissatisfied customer is obligated to do. Thus being the case, we are making the following recommendations for the survival of your establishment.

1. Hire quality employees. It is not enough to simply have warm bodies that clock in and stand before customers taking orders or taking money. Your employees are a reflection of you. If they present themselves in an intolerable and unclean manner, we as consumers have no choice but to think that your business is intolerable and unclean. If you cannot hire good help, or train your help to become the best, then your business will simply not survive.

2. Treat every customer with the utmost respect. Customers are the reason you exist. You must emphasize this to all of your employees. If a staff member does not understand the need for customers, you do not need that staff member. This includes some very basic tasks such as: greeting people with a pleasant attitude, thanking them for patronizing your business, asking them if they were served properly, and speaking clearly when interacting with customers. Have your staff stand when customers enter and immediately ask how they can be of service.

3. *Always have product for your customers. It hurts your business more than you know when consumers request service or products that you fail to provide, without a logical explanation. This may require you to better manage your inventory or reevaluate how you can provide service in a more timely manner. If you repeatedly fail to provide products or services, customers will find what they need from your competitors.*

4. *Your staff should give customers all of their time and attention. Keep your employees from talking on the phone, checking their pagers, or having casual conversations when customers are awaiting service.*

5. *Demonstrate good leadership. Your employees can only be as good as the management and leadership of the establishment. This means your managers must have a clear understanding of what it takes to have a productive and profitable day. They must know how to motivate as well as discipline the staff. A manager should be the one of the best employees in your company.*

6. *Sacrifice for the good of your business. If changes in employment need to take place, or people need to be replaced, don't be afraid to do so. Don't be reluctant to sacrifice scheduling in order to train or recruit better people. If hiring better people means paying a higher salary, realize that inferior employees will hurt your profits over a long period of time, as well as tarnish the image of your business.*

7. *Ask your customers for feedback. Surveys are a good way of finding out how people feel about your services, your prices, and your products.*

We sincerely hope that you will consider these recommendations carefully. We are sure that you as a business leader want to be successful, just as we want you to contribute to the community. In fact, we are so confident that you will apply these recommendations, we have placed you on the consideration list for next year's grant. We have already selected as this year's grant recipient an outstanding business that exemplifies quality products and outstanding customer service. Should you have any questions or concerns regarding information contained within this correspondence, please don't hesitate to call. We exist to help you.

Best Regards,

Karen Batch, MBA
Community Enrichment Coordinator

Randall flipped the letter around hoping to find his name next to the words *Congratulations* or *You've been selected*. There were no more words and no more pages. He grabbed the phone and jammed his finger into the phone ten times, hitting the numbers shown on the company's letterhead.

"This is Karen Batch."

"I got yo' damn letter."

"Good...uh, I'm glad. I hope you received it well because we meant..."

"What is this?"

"What is what?"

"This letter. Why couldn't you just call me and tell me who won?"

"Mr. Harvey, that letter is not about winning or losing. It's about us helping one another and improving."

"You must be crazy! If you was gon' help, you should have sent a check. I don't need no letter tellin' me—"

"For your information. Mr. Harvey, that letter was drafted for me by a mystery shopper and we sent it to several business. I'm actually at my office now and getting ready to send out more copies to other businesses. I had a bad experience at a McDonald's the other day and the owner of that franchise is getting a copy. Don't feel like you're the only one who—"

"Does this mean the only Black business on the final evaluation ain't gon' get the money?"

"Well, that's one perspective. But, as you are aware, the consideration was not based on race. However, another minority-owned business was selected."

"You know what? I shoulda known you was a damn sell-out. What the hell am I supposed to do now? I closed the restaurant for remodelin' 'cause after them Mexicans poisoned everybody wasn't nobody else in the runnin'. As soon as—"

"Uh...you can hold that crap right there," Karen interjected, her professional demeanor vacillating.

"Let me tell you one thing—in fact, let me tell you a few things. This ain't about me. It's about the community. You're lucky your rundown grease bowl made it this far. For your information, I wasn't the one mystery shopping. One of my evaluators told me about their experience at your place and called it a joke. Do you hear me! They called it a *joke*! And this was *after* I warned you to fix your problems. Now, I could've written you off and not sent the letter, but I didn't. And this is how I get treated. Nobody told you to remodel your place and certainly nobody gave you any indication that you were going to get the grant. You call my office and offend me? Mr. Harvey, you got me mixed up with somebody that plays that game, because I—"

"Who you give to, huh? Who you give it to? Them Asians, didn't you? Gave it to the Asians. I know you did 'cause I know you."

"You obviously don't know me very well because we awarded the grant to Mr. Santos' establishment."

"What! You did *what*?"

"Mr. Harvey, they know how to run a business. Their scores were so much higher than anyone else's—"

"Them Mexicans killed my boy and you give them a million dollars! What the hell is wrong wit' chu! You done lost yo' damn mind! They killed my boy!"

"Mr. Harvey, you need to calm down. I will not be spoken to on the phone like this. I—"

"I ain't got nothin' else to say on this damn phone! I'm on my way over there! What I got to do, I'm gon' do it in person, you mutha—!"

"*What* did you say? Mr. Harvey, don't you dare threaten me! In fact…"

Karen pressed the end button on her phone, furious at the disrespect. Her chest heaved up and down, lungs struggling to transport angry air. Hair stood up on her neck. She cursed between grinding teeth and pressed lips. The phone beeped again. This time she would not let him get a word in. She wouldn't listen to a single breath. Karen pressed the talk button without looking at the screen.

"You do *not* call me and talk to me like you're crazy! Come over here if you want to and I'll have the police jack you up in the lobby. Who the hell do you think you are?"

"Um… your husband?"

"Ethan?"

"Yeah. Honey, what's goin' on? You're not still at your office, are you?"

"I didn't know it was you," she replied, her chest heaving again, this time with relief at the sound of her husband's cordial voice. "I'm still here. This idiot who was being considered for the grant, Mr. Harvey—"

"The guy whose son died?"

"Yeah, him. He called here irate! He threatened me."

"What!"

"He said something about coming over here or something like that."

"Really?"

"Yeah."

"I'm only three minutes away from you now. I'll take care of it."

"No. Don't worry about that. There's a security guard here on Saturdays. Why are you on your way here, anyway?"

"You need to see something. And you don't need to be working today anyhow. Can you wrap up what you're doing, save it for Monday?"

"I suppose. What is it?"

"You remember that flier you showed me a while ago and how we thought Santos might have gotten the construction bid?"

"Yeah."

"Well, I found out through the grapevine that they got it and the project was completed a month ago. There's a grand opening today and you're not gonna believe what I just saw."

"What is it?"

"I'll be pulling into your parking lot by the time you get downstairs. Come on out. I'll say this, though."

"What?" Karen asked.

"Memorial Drive just got a facelift."

Chapter Fifteen

Business as Un-usual

It was the largest banner anyone had ever seen on Memorial Drive. It was second in size only to the huge billboard high above the newly renovated building, screaming the words *Grand Opening*. Someone had obviously done all the right research, or hired the right people. The letters were the optimum height for drivers to take notice just in time to enter the parking lot if their attention had been grabbed. Someone had known that bright red against a dark background would draw eyes toward the message. Human factors in engineering was an actual college course and someone had apparently aced all the tests.

A remote radio broadcast was taking place in front of the building. There were, in fact, two radio stations, both with buzzwords common to urban ears. *Power. Hot. Kiss. Hits.* Large, air-filled giants stood over the parking lot, falling and rising causing even more commotion. Balloons floated high trying to escape skinny ribbon strings holding them captive. The yellow, red, blue, and green latex ovals danced and jerked whichever way the wind wanted. No one could pass by and ignore the extravaganza — exactly what the proprietor had hoped. If the rubberneckers were curious enough, they would stop. If they stopped, they would inquire. If they inquired, they would participate. If they participated, they were trapped.

Cars were pouring into the parking lot. Some entrances had lines of cars spilling back into the streets. Radio listeners driving home in their cars had, no doubt, been enticed by the radio personalities offering some gift pack or concert tickets, or whatever made people jump from cars asking what they had won.

Randall was one of those curious listeners. He was speeding to Karen's office hoping to influence her with his physical presence. Instead, he was lured into the parking lot when he heard the bouncing, energetic voice offer something most people could not refuse. Half a block away he noticed the attraction. The research had worked on him too; the large letters, the billboards, the extreme hype. There was so much to take in, he didn't notice Karen and her husband pull up behind him. Once in the parking lot, they drove to separate locations in search for parking spaces, which were rapidly disappearing.

Karen pointed to a space, urging Ethan to grab it quickly. She was anxious to see what was going on, as was everyone else. Their car radio was tuned into the live remote. As they exited the car, they heard the broadcast continue live and in person.

"This is Frank Cameron and I'm coming to you live from the newly opened Culture Complex on Memorial Drive. We'll be here all day. I would ordinarily give somethin' away to the first person who comes up to me and says they heard me in their car, but I can't. You know why? Because everything here is free! That's right, you heard me. Today only, at this grand openin', for the next four hours, every service and every product is *free* to the public.

"I gotta listener right here. Come on up, grab the mic and tell all the people your name."

"My name Quydeesha, I'm from Decata, I ain't no hata, can't nobody do it greata!"

"Whew, slow down girl! You off da chain, ain't cha?"

"Baby, I'm off da bulldozer."

"Go ahead on wit' yo' bad self. Tell everybody what you gon' get at the Culture Complex."

"I'm gettin' it all! It's free and I'm gettin' it all. Soon as it open, I'm gettin' everything they got."

"All right, then. Save some for everybody else. Everybody come on down right now! We are just two minutes from the formal grand openin' of the Culture Complex. Any minute now we will...wait. I think..."

The broadcaster stopped as the front doors were uncovered from the inside. A signal was given to both radio stations and the volume of their music was lowered.

From inside the building, trumpet music blared as though royalty was about to appear. The doors were pushed open as the line of people moved toward the entrance. Suddenly, they were pushed back by a rushing billow of steam from a smoke machine. As the smoke subsided, employees dressed in new uniforms walked outside in single file lines. Each of them waved to the crowd and grinned with red carpet movie premiere smiles. The army of employees seemed to be endless. They were all grouped according to position and expertise.

There was a line of twenty men wearing red and blue smocks with an embroidered image of a barbershop pole and scissors on their left breast pocket. Each of them had a pair of electric clippers held high in their right hands. There was a line of thirty-five women with pink and blue smocks, a picture of hair rollers, scissors, and nail polish stitched across the front. They were all holding curling irons or nail files and smiling just like the barbers.

Next was a line of twelve young boys and girls — smiling, of course. They were wearing waterproof orange jumpsuits and holding large sponges in each hand.

The parade of happy workers continued with a line of ten men dressed in checkered pants and white jackets, chef hats atop their heads. Towels were hanging from their waists. The towels were embroidered with the words *Country Cooking For Your Soul*.

After the army of seventy-seven workers had emerged, a gentleman dressed in a dark blue three-piece suit walked through the doors. He nodded to the radio broadcaster, who then rushed over to the impeccably dressed man and gave him the microphone. He spoke with the clarity and diction of a highly educated and polished scholar.

"Ladies and gentlemen. People of the community. Welcome to the Culture Complex, where everything you need is under one roof. For the next four hours, to show you how well we can serve you, everything here is free!"

The crowd erupted with cheers and shouts. The people moved closer, anxious to get in.

"So get your car hand-washed by our energetic youngsters, your nails sculpted by our highly trained technicians, your hair cut by our master barbers, or your hair styled by our licensed cosmetologists. Or enjoy our delicious home cooked country buffet. Have a great evening—it's on the house!" This time the man disappeared into the building and was followed by the crowd and each of the seventy-seven smiling, enthused, and qualified—Korean employees.

Chapter Sixteen

Complex Cultures

The well-dresser speaker was a shepherd and the patrons in search of free products were being herded like sheep. Karen and Ethan were amongst the flock, pushing and shoving their way to see the building that had been under wraps for months. Large tarps had covered the exterior during the re-modeling, allowing no one to see what was coming to the community. Like the others, Karen and Ethan were amazed once inside.

Comfortable barber chairs were aligned in two precise rows. Television screens were mounted on both sides of each row, suspended from the ceiling. Customers could see the screens no matter which way their chairs were turned. Cartoons were on some of the sets, music videos on others, CNN and ESPN on the remaining ones.

In the women's salon, each chair had its own individual magazine rack and small stereo speakers. Even the dreaded wash-and-rinse chairs and hair dryer chairs were designed with comfort in mind. There were stereo speakers in each of these, as well as a control module. While selecting a radio station or playing a CD, women could activate the vibrating back massage inside the chair. Large air ducts above whirled and buzzed, drawing the toxic smells out of the air.

Plants and framed art decorated the salon, adding to the pleasant environment. Karen noticed the padded reclining chairs in the manicure section. Each chair had adjustable armrests — women had to simply lie still and let the chair move while getting both pedicures and manicures. There were television sets placed throughout this area, just like the barber shop section. It was more comfortable than most homes.

Smells from the restaurant wafted in and out of corridors. Those waiting could easily have been drawn to the aromas calling them over, pulling them in to have a taste.

"Can you believe this?" Karen asked Ethan.

"I can and I can't," Ethan answered. "I never imagined somebody else would come in and serve us our own culture better than we can."

"How long have we been going to barbershops and beauty parlors?"

"Forget that. How long have we been cooking our own soul food?"

Karen looked out at the spectacle, once more noticing something new at every corner. Finally she turned to Ethan and said, "I don't think it's gonna work."

"Why not?"

"You've had the same barber for years because you like the way he cuts. And my girlfriend has had Celeste do her hair for as long as I can remember. If it's one thing Black folks don't play with, it's their hair," she answered.

"I think you're wrong, honey."

"Why's that?" she asked.

"Because those..." Ethan was interrupted by an employee handing out fliers.

A small, polite Korean woman said, fighting her accent, "Excuse-a-me. Here are da cost for servahces. Tank you fah coming."

"Thank you," said Ethan. "Because, honey," he continued, reading the flier. "Well, here's another reason why it'll work right here. My God! How are they making a profit with prices like this?"

"This can't be right. These have got to be mistakes," Karen said.

The two were silent for a moment while they read the information.

Personal Care
*Haircuts $5 everyday
Mustache & beard trim free with haircut, $2 without.
Wash, cut, style, set $25 everyday
(free if you're not done in two hours)*

*Manicure $7
French Manicure $10
Pedicure $7.50
Polish change $1.00
Nail art starting at $1.75
Paraffin hand treatment $2.50
Paraffin foot treatment $ 5.00*

*Full set of acrylic nails $10-$20
Nail repairs (after 2 weeks) $1.75
Nail removal with manicure $15.00*

*Eyebrow waxing $1.75
Eyebrow Arch $1.75*

*Our products and services comply with **all** current North
American health regulations.*

Restaurant—Lunch & Dinner Buffet
*All you can eat everyday $5
Meat & two vegetables $3.50
Kids twelve and under eat free*

Car Wash
Hand car wash interior and exterior $7

"Uh, Karen. I don't know about all of this manicure, cut and washin' stuff, but you can't get a professional five-dollar haircut nowhere in Atlanta."

"These are way below any nail or hair salon I've every seen. It's gotta make you wonder about the quality."

"I know somebody who's not worried about the quality."

"Who's that?"

"All of those people that just filled up every single one of those chairs."

Randall walked briskly around the complex, checking out people's faces. He was trying to determine if they were as astonished as he was. For a few moments he, too, was mesmerized by the rows of televisions in the barbershop, but he was angered by the notion that it was not his business all these people were flocking to. He thought about the letter he'd received, how insulted he was. Now, looking around at the marvel, he thought there may be some truth to it. The aromas captivated him, just as they had the others, and then frustrated him because they weren't the smell of his own specially seasoned fish. Randall peered into the restaurant and saw his inevitable demise. People were laughing, smiling, licking their fingers, and running back to the line for more.

The well-dressed announcer was walking toward Randall, shaking hands, helping people find their way.

"Hello. Welcome to the Culture Complex. May I help you with something?" he asked, beaming a grin at Randall.

"It ain't gon' work."

"I beg your pardon?" The announcer asked.

"This fancy setup you got here ain't gon' be around for long."

"I'm sorry, sir. Have you had a bad experience? We want to ensure you are one hundred percent satisfied."

"I ain't satisfied 'cause you ain't gon' serve me. Don't nobody want none of this. See all of these folks in here? They ain't gon' be here next week or the week after that. Watch what I say. You'll be closed by Christmas."

"Sir, have we met before?"

"Nah we ain't met! Ain't seen you in this community until today! That's why you ain't gon' make it."

"I'm Daniel Lee, president of Lee & Sons, LLC. My mother owns a beauty supply store a few blocks down. And you are?"

"Randall Harvey and you don't need to..."

"Ah yes. Mr. Harvey of the delightful Fish Nets. Eaten at your place once or twice. *Great* catfish. Best I've ever had, I swear. Told my chefs, if they couldn't prepare catfish as good as Fish Nets on the corner, don't even try. Honest, Mr. Harvey."

Randall was confused. He had at first wanted to fight this man. Wanted a reason to burn the building to the ground. But instead he now wanted to shake his hand. The words *thank you* were almost pulled from his vengeful jaws. He visually searched the man, looking for a foothold to intensify his assault. All he found was a custom-tailored navy blue pinstriped suit and baby blue wing-collar shirt, brilliantly contrasting with an orange silk tie and coordinating orange pocket handkerchief. Cufflinks sparkled with each hand gesture. Randall, still wanting to admonish the man, was now fighting admiration.

"Well...I appreciate that. But just the same it ain't gon' work. Might be around a little longer than Christmas. After that it's goin' downhill. I can promise you that. People 'round here won't take too much to folks that ain't they own. You and yo' mama can pack up and get ready to leave."

Daniel Lee was changing hues. The smooth yellow-tinted skin was transforming into dull red.

"How can you be so arrogan—" He caught himself. "I mean, so sure, Mr. Harvey?"

"I know these things. Just like I know that Mexican place won't be open for much longer. People think it will, but it won't."

"Mexican place. Are you referring to La Familia? Mr. Santos' establishment?"

"Yeah that's the one. That damn place gon' close down whether y'all know it or not. And you gon' be next. Why don't you go open up a Chinese restaurant somewhere. That's all y'all good for."

Daniel Lee fought back the words boiling in his gut and rising up his throat. His cordial demeanor hid the desire to lash out with insulting profanity. Instead, he flanked his enemy.

"Mr. Harvey, would you mind stepping into my office? I have something to show you."

"What the hell I wanna come to your office for? Ain't nothin' up there I need to see."

"Well, in my office is the only way that you will close down Mr. Santos' establishment." Randall's mouth dropped. For once, he was speechless. "In my office, Mr. Harvey, is a way for your business to make more money than you've ever seen. It's just this way. Won't you follow me?"

The two rose up a flight of steps leading to a large room where the walls were made of glass. It overlooked the entire complex from different sides of the room. What had once been a security overlook had been converted into a state-of-the-art eagle's nest, complete with a full bath and small bedroom. Clearly, this was were Daniel worked — and lived, when late nights mandated he do so.

Old pictures in new frames were placed on tables and shelves all over the room. There were black and white photos of Asian women with large baskets on their heads standing in rice fields. Old pictures of Asian couples holding infants, all dressed in their best, newly acquired American clothes. An old color

Polaroid of a large Asian family standing in front of a house next to a real estate sign, the word SOLD in large print. Pictures were everywhere and not one had less than three people. Most of the snapshots were of at least eight people.

Degrees were framed and adhered to the glass wall behind a gigantic desk. University of Georgia, Georgia Tech, Emory — the state's own walk of academic fame, Georgia's self-proclaimed Ivy League.

"Have a seat, Mr. Harvey. May I pour you a drink?" He reached for a cut-glass decanter.

"Look, man, don't try to wine me and dine me up here in this fancy suite. Just tell me what I want to know. You need to bring some boxes up here so you can start packing when you go out of business."

Daniel sighed, shook his head, grinned, and sighed once more.

"Mr. Harvey, let me ask you something. What was the projected revenue for the first year of your business plan?"

"The what?"

"Who were your top competitors when you developed your business model?"

"What you talkin' about?"

"How long before you make profits based on your capital start-up cost?"

"Look here, I don't use them fancy business practices much, but what I — "

"Mr. Harvey, forgive my brash sentiments, but you're a dinosaur and a lucky one at that. How dare you come into my place of business, insult me, my family, my heritage and make these threats."

Randall was shocked. The polite gentleman had become an aggressive demon. He was stunned into silence.

"I'll tell you what you need to know. What you need to know is the Culture Complex will be around much longer than Christmas. In fact we're projected to be around for the next ten years, growing by twenty percent every year. What you need to know is that tomorrow, there will be just as many people in here as there are today. What you need to know is that we've scouted every single business that offers the same product or service that we provide. And what we've found is that businesses like yours have alienated their patrons by giving poor customer service. Take a look down there, Mr. Harvey. Take a good look.

"See those *African-American* women having their hair styled and braided for free by qualified and trained professionals? Do you see that there is not one single empty chair? What do think is going to happen when they are pleased with the end result, tell all of their friends, and find out they can't get that type of fast, friendly service at our prices anywhere else?

"Look over here, Mr. Harvey. Do you see all of these African-American men getting their haircuts? Quickly, without the barbers talking on the telephone or holding a conversation while the customer sits around in the chair waiting for him to finish. Do you honestly think that all of your people get their haircuts just to sit around and hear people talk? Now this is critical. We understand that the camaraderie of men is a vital part of the barbershop atmosphere, but we let the *customers* carry on the conversation. We don't inconvenience them by talking instead of cutting. Take a look. See how the men in chairs are joking and laughing. The barbers are *working*. What do you think will happen when those master barbers give a great haircut for five dollars?

"Look over here at this side. See all of those women getting manicures and pedicures? Do you see? Now you and I both know that's a business we took from you a long time ago. We've just consolidated it under one roof, at a great price.

"Did you see this side over here, Mr. Harvey? Look at all of these people standing in line for food. Not just normal food, but *great* food. Great southern soul food. Your food, Mr. Harvey. Made the way your people have made it for years. But if you look closely, you can see the smile on the faces of our employees, and look at that family right there, they're smiling back to the cashier. You know what the cashier is saying? She's saying *Thank you for coming. Please enjoy your meal and come back soon. If you need anything else, just ask.* Do you know how I know, Mr. Harvey? Because I wrote the script and everyone says that. They're saying it now and they will continue saying it long past Christmas.

"What do they say to customers at your place, Mr. Harvey? I'll tell you what they say because I've been there. After I give people at your place money — money to put food on your table, keep your business open, and sustain your family? You know what they say? All they say is '*Next!*' They don't say please, they don't say thank you, they don't say welcome, they don't say hi. Sometimes they don't say anything at all. Sometimes they just close the drive-thru window. That's why we'll be here way past Christmas.

"And of course you saw this, right? Over here. This line of cars. Those are going into the carwash. The carwash where we'll hand wash in ten minutes or less, for a much better price than people pulling into a parking lot with a pressure washer and large container of water.

"You could have done this a long time ago. You and all of your people. My mother and sister told me about this area, but I just didn't believe it until I saw it. Seventeen hot wing stands within a five mile strip and none of you had the brains to combine all of that money and those resources into one large, extremely profitable restaurant? Nine people washing cars on one street and those guys couldn't merge to buy or rent a building, share the market instead compete for business? Five Jamaican restaurants within two miles of each other and they won't consolidate? Quite frankly, it's baffling to me, while at the same time, amusing, but also very sad. You folks have suffered a long and hard history. You deserve much better than this. So, I'd like to help you a little bit." Daniel's sermon was a delicate balance of sarcasm and condescension.

"You see, we'll be here a while, Mr. Harvey. Something tells me that all of those 'fancy' business practices just might be helpful after all. But you, sir, they wouldn't help you even if you tried. That's why I'm offering you a once-in-a-lifetime deal. No, as a matter of fact, I'm offering you a *life-saving* deal. What I will offer you is a position on my staff as an assistant seafood chef."

"A what!" Randall exclaimed. The demotion from entrepreneur to hired cook snapped him out of his paralysis.

"It seems, Mr. Harvey, try as we might, we just haven't been able to duplicate your taste. Now, don't get me wrong, our seafood is great, but we want your taste and I believe in eliminating the competition—one way or another. You can join us or you can wait until we steal all of your customers."

"Ain't no way!" Randall yelled.

"Before you begin another of your tirades, think about what you're doing. I've already talked to other businesses and they're taking me up on whatever offer I give them. This is business, Mr. Harvey. You're in it to make money, not lose it. Look, we've got cooperation from the small bakery down the street. It would have been two months tops before we crushed that little old lady making sweet potato pie and red velvet cake. The hot wing restaurant across the street

143

is coming on board. Heaven knows they wouldn't have made it to the end of the month. Even La Familia is allowing us to license their name and products. We'll be sort of a small franchise for them. It's a win-win situation for everyone. That's where you come in. Our head chef has a wonderful idea. He's calling it a 'culture combination.' His plan is to take the best dishes of your establishment and La Familia. We're going to name it Catfish Quesadillas. Isn't that great?"

"Are you crazy?" Randall exploded. "Hell nawh! Man, get out my way! You got to be out yo' mind. You done lost it!" Randall said, rushing for the door.

"Mr. Harvey. *You* have lost it! Your people have lost it and you won't get it back! You're going backwards!"

Randall's hand was on the doorknob, but he couldn't turn it. He was drawn to the brutal truth continuing to swallow him in this room.

"You don't see it, but you're fighting a losing battle. Got all the wrong weapons. You're fighting with hopes and dreams and we're fighting with a mindset and a way of life. You pay your family to work at your place while we have been working for our families for only a place to stay and leftover food from the restaurant. We've been running businesses without a payroll. Your children use their wages to pay rent in their apartments while we were all living in the same apartment. Money that would have been paid in wages went right back into the restaurant to grow the business.

"You laugh at the Hispanics like the Santos family because six, eight, or ten of them are cramped in one vehicle going to work. That's one car payment for ten people, whereas ten of your people have one car note each. Mr. Santos' family comes from a place where washing dishes feeds a family of five. But your people, your young people see this as a disgraceful job. Meanwhile, the grandfather and father of Mr. Santos washed dishes and shared a small home with three other families. And now Mr. Santos has a thriving restaurant and a construction company — that renovated this building, I might add. Mr. Harvey, how many of your people will live together under one roof with other families to better themselves? Or better yet, how many of your people will live under one roof with extended members of their own family?

"It's a mindset, Harvey. You understand? A mindset of sacrifice. You know what I saw when I was an intern at Motorola? I saw a Hispanic custodian getting ready for lunch. People used to line up in front of the microwave ovens waiting to heat their food. This little Hispanic lady stood in front of the microwave getting ready to heat her lunch and I watched her as she put eight sandwiches in the microwave. Eight sandwiches! I followed her because I wanted to see her eat all of those sandwiches. Turns out, she was warming up the sandwiches for all of the other Hispanics sitting at her table. Even when they weren't working, they were working together. While all of these other people — most of them your people—stood in line with their individual sandwiches, the Hispanics were enjoying lunch, together.

"It's your mindset, Harvey. That's the only way you'll close Santos down. That's the only way you'll survive. It's how we've come to be so successful so quickly." Daniel Lee's face suddenly took on a scolding look, exploding as though he'd been struggling to remain civil. "A way of thinking that's been around for centuries and we're going to keep it around—way past Christmas."

"You'll call me later, when your family is looking for a job. You'll call me then. Or you can wait and have your grandson work for my grandson. Now, get out of my office."

Chapter Seventeen

Trading Traitors

Now that the Culture Complex had been opened, Juan Santos could concentrate more of his time on La Familia and, more importantly, dealing with issues of family treason. Renovation of the complex had demanded most of his time. Besides being a confidential project, it had generated over two million dollars in revenue for his small construction company. It was the project needed to elevate his business to the next plateau. Juan was growing tired of mediocrity and wanted more for his establishment. Wanted to be a business mogul, wanted power and respect. Wanted to be more than just a Hispanic immigrant living the American Dream. He wanted the dream in surround sound and high definition.

With the revenue and reputation of the Culture Complex under his belt, Juan could venture into land development—the current Atlanta gold mine. On the average seven thousand people were moving to Atlanta every month now. Juan wanted to do more than simply serve them quesadillas, cut their grass, and repair their homes. He wanted to build those homes. Payoff for renovation of the Culture Complex was so bountiful, Juan had forgotten all about the million-dollar grant. Until he got the call.

"Juan Santos speaking."

"Mr. Santos, Karen Batch here. How are you?"

"Karen, hello! I fine how are you? Good to hear you."

"Fine, thanks for asking. I've got some great news to share."

"Okay."

"Our mystery shoppers evaluated La Familia and it received the highest evaluation of all the other businesses that were considered."

"That great! Oh, that wonderful news!"

"Well, that's not the good news. The good news is that you are the recipient of the community improvement grant."

"What! Are you joking? Really? You are serious?"

"Yes, I am very serious. Congratulations—Hello? Hello?"

Juan dropped the phone in his excitement and Karen could hear him shouting in the background. She could hear him delivering the news and other people had begun shouting along with him. Footsteps hurried and grew louder as Juan rushed back to the receiver.

Juan said, breathing hard, "Hello? Karen? I sorry. I had to run and say, eh, the good news. Oh this is great day for us!"

"I'm sure it is. We're going to set up a press conference next week, at which time we will present the first installment of the check."

"Oh, great!"

"Now, we'd also like to use your business as a model for the community. Perhaps arrange tours for other people thinking of starting restaurants, get you active with the Chamber of Commerce and things of that nature. How do you feel about those ideas?"

"However I can help is great."

"Good, I figured you would be very cooperative. So, any plans for the funding? Add on to your building, new equipment? You can use it any way you see fit as long as it's for the business we evaluated. For instance, it couldn't be used for your construction business, but additions to the restaurant are perfectly allowable. How's that going, by the way? Maybe we can evaluate that business for the next funding consideration." Karen tried to disguise an inquiry about his participation in Culture Complex

"Oh no. No need for that. We are doing, eh, well in that. We just finish big project called Culture Complex. Now we have grant, I no have to use construction money for La Familia. This is great for me."

"I visited the Culture Complex. You all did a great job on that. How'd you hear about the project?"

"I talk to Daniel Lee long time ago. He talk to me about bidding and I tell him we have the lowest bid of anybody."

"So he told you what the other bids were?"

"No, no, no! That not good business. I told him we have lowest ,eh, bid because our workers are family. They know we pay small ,eh, wages now for bigger wages for our children. We always have lowest bid, and best schedule."

"Hmmm. that's interesting," Karen said, scratching her head, realizing her husband had never had a chance. "We'll definitely have to take a look at your construction side during the next evaluation. This should come at a great time for you — now you can earn back some of your restaurant's business. Whatever came of the investigation?"

"Karen," he said his voice decreasing in volume. "I hate to say, but I have bad people in my family. They have betray me."

"Huh?"

"Someone betray me and help people try to hurt La Familia."

"Are you saying what I think you are?"

"Yes. I know who do this thing and people will know."

"Have you told the police?"

"I will handle my own. Then I will—" Juan was interrupted by a knock on the door.

A head poked in. "Soy yo," the man said.

Juan gave the man a menacing frown. He spit on the floor and said, "Ingles!"

"It me," the man said timidly.

"Karen, I must go now. There is…eh, traitor in my office I must execute."

"That's pretty funny. I've had a few folks around here that I thought were traitors. Never thought about executing them. I'll have to try that," she said, chuckling, waiting for Juan's laughter. It never came.

"I serious," Juan said. We talk later."

He hung up the phone and kept his hand clutched around the receiver. The man was still hesitating in the doorway.

"Come in, sit down, no talking, understand?"

"Si."

Juan quickly turned his head toward the man, who was now approaching a chair.

"Yes," the man said, changing his language. Perhaps it was a good sign, Juan caring enough about his future to insist that he continue practicing the native language. Still, he was unsure why Juan had arranged the meeting, though he did have his suspicions.

Juan rose from his chair, arms folded, each footstep toward the man slow and intentional. He stood behind him and placed a hand on his shoulder.

"How hab you been?"

"O.K."

"You sure? We not seen you since you quit."

"I okay."

Juan raised his hand and dropped it back down on the man's shoulder. The man grimaced with slight pain and became nervous about the increasing power of Juan's hands.

"I think you are mad at us. No?"

"No, I okay. Not work for you again."

"Yes, you told me when you quit."

"My familia was here long time. I work hard eby day. You should give best job to me," said the man.

"Yes, I know you worked harder. Harder than people at site. But you did not work hard on your ingles. I say to you long time ago. you must speak good ingles to get foreman job. It mean more money, but more, eh, responsibility. I say this each month, but you not get better with ingles. You not try to learn more, you not work hard the right way."

"No, you no give me job so Jorge can have job. You want to give foreman job to you son. Jorge, eh, not need job. Jorge es, eh, you son and, eh get what you have. Eh, money, house, eh, business. I need job. We hab new baby, and want to, eh, build house. You hab nice house. We want nice house."

"It take time. It take time for me to get nice house. I get nice house for more people to move from Mexico and start new life. I not selfish like you!" This time Juan raised his hand above the man's shoulder and descended with a demolishing fist.

"¡Carajo de mienda!" he said, unleashing profanity.

"See! Still no ingles. If you did what I say, you would have job. But you not do it. But you do this to me!"

Juan raised and dropped his hand once more, this time with even more force.

Juan retrieved the remote control from his pocket and smashed the play button. White lines danced across the television for a few seconds, then disappeared. As the man watched the screen, Juan looked at him. Watching for remorse, watching for evil, watching for a reason to hurt him.

The video camera had been mounted high above the door to capture any movements near the back entrance. What was intended as a device to see which delivery was arriving had now become the means of proof. For a while, the picture showed only the walkway leading to the door. Time elapsed and the two employees were seen unlocking, then entering the building. Before he saw it, the man knew what was next. He turned his head, pretending that there was a more important object somewhere about the room, looking around for anything. A vent, a nail on the wall waiting for its fateful meeting with a frame, a book waiting for someone to reach the page where it would remain open on its own without being pressed down by reading hands.

"Look at it!" Look what you did!" Juan demanded, slamming the man's shoulder again.

"Aggh!" he yelled, louder this time, bending at the hips to give himself an excuse to look at the floor.

Juan clasped a huge lock of the man's black hair in his hand and yanked his head up, forcing him to look at the screen. And he saw it. It was all too familiar again, the cold temperature, the curling smoke from cold breath, the fears of getting caught by police. But never once thinking that it might have come to this. Verbal and physical torture at the hands of a friend.

The mistake had been looking back. They should have just run out the door, never looking back, and running till either they were caught or exhausted. But instead, both of the men looked back inside to see if they were being followed. And that's where Juan paused the picture. The man was looking at himself. History and the present staring at each other. There in the frozen frame he also saw his future.

The man closed his eyes, squeezing back tears of betrayal. Juan's grip was so tight his hand began to shake, but he would not let the man turn his head on the sight the way he had turned his back on Juan's trust. He could feel the follicles in the man's head deforming, stretching to their limit just before extraction. The man wanted to scream, but the pain of deceit silenced him. Juan finally loosed him, shoving his head to the floor.

"Lo siento. Lo siento. I sorry," the man said, apologizing.

Juan moved back to his desk, breathing hard from the intense exertion. He plunged into his chair, looking at the man slow to rise from the floor.

"Are you ready to go back to Juarez? Are you ready to take your family back to the streets and beg? Your boy can spit fire for pennies. Are you ready?"

"No, Juan. Please help us. I need, eh, job," he replied, groveling." Please help my familia."

"Why? Why should I? You try to hurt my family. Why should I help ju?"

"I will no do again. Eber. I will no do again. I will do, eh, what you say."

"I know you will. First you will find this man with you there," Juan said pointing to the screen. "And you will bring him to justice. People must know that La Familia is clean. I will help how I can after they find out who have done this. If you hab problems, I will take care of your family forever. It my promise to you. But now you know what you must do? Understand?"

"Si, eh, yes," he replied with a cowered head, fully knowing what he did now was not for him but for future generations. Slowly, he walked over to the screen that had revealed him and his partner in crime...and pushed eject.

Chapter Eighteen

Reality

Only a month after the Culture Complex had opened, businesses were starting to close. Those that weren't closing and had no loyal clientele were hurting badly. La Familia was making a rapid recovery, but Randall was suffering. The money he'd lost by closing the restaurant would have allowed him to stay afloat. As it was, he was drowning quickly. Veronica found herself still swimming in grief. Corey had taken on another job to help with money working nights at an electronics factory in Gwinnett County, forty minutes from the restaurant. Oftentimes he found himself sleeping over at the home of a co-worker in order to avoid the late drive home. At least that's what he told Randall.

Despite his extra income, he was still unable to splurge beyond necessities. He could buy groceries, but not steaks. He could buy gasoline, but not a car wash. He could buy an oil change, but not a badly needed engine repair.

Corey's cell phone was scheduled to be disconnected at week's end. Fortunately, it was the middle of the week when his car broke down on the interstate.

"Pops, I need some help," he said to the other end of a phone filled with static.

"Oh, Corey, I been meaning to sit down and talk with ya, son. I really have. With the business goin' the way it has, it's just slipped my mind."

"I know, Pops. But that's not what I need right now. I need a ride home. My car stopped last night on the way to work. My boy came and picked me up so I wouldn't be late, but he couldn't bring me all the way back home this mornin'. You think you could — "

"Where you at?"

"The car is on highway 316, up near Duluth. I'm at the gas station right off the Sugarloaf exit."

"No problem, I'm pullin' into the oil change place now. After I leave here, I'm on the way. You eat yet?"

"Nawh."

"I'll pick somethin' on the way. We can talk about whatever you wanted to on the way back."

"Thanks, Pops."

"No problem, boy. I'm gone take care of you."

"I know. That's what I want to talk to you about."

Corey rubbed his thumb over the end button of his phone and waited for his father.

Randall pulled into the oil change franchise and waited to wheel his car into the service area. He listened to the radio while waiting and noticed that he'd heard the entire last half of a popular tune and no one had greeted him. The song ended and he heard a commercial for the Culture Complex. Catchy music, jazzy and quick played before the jingle began:

The Culture Complex
Where customers can rest
Quality, Pride, and Service
Is what you'll expect
At the Culture Complex

Sound bites of customer's testimonials with an urban flair followed next:

— *Culture Complex is the bomb! My lil' boy got his hairuh cut while I got my toes did and it was all less than thirty dollas! Culture Complex is the bess!*

— *I was really surprised. I stopped here because I was running late and I must admit I'll take my time gettin' here on the next trip. I was in and out like that. Culture Complex is best.*

— *Yo! Dem wings is off da chain! I tell my girl to gets me some of them joints whenever she get her hair did. And she have money left over after so they hook her nails up. Culture Complex is the best!*

A narrator trailed in after the testimonials with a resonating baritone voice.

At the Culture Complex, you'll be treated to the best service anywhere. The quality and cost of our products is unmatched and it's all under one roof. What more can you ask for? Well, whatever you ask for, we'll provide it. Stop by and see us today. We're located at 27269 Memorial Drive. We open early and close late.

And then the jingle again. Randall felt ill. It wasn't until this moment that he realized he'd never had a radio ad, or any type of advertising for his business. Thoughts of Daniel Lee's offer haunted him. He kept thinking of the words. Catfish Quesadillas. The term meant his surrender and his eventual defeat. It meant that he'd lost what little foothold he'd had on his business. Randall then realized that he'd heard half a song, plus a full commercial, and still had not been greeted.

He smashed the horn and the sound rousted a worker out of the office. The man looked in Randall's direction, shook his head, and stormed out of the office in a frantic pace.

"Keyshawn! Hey yo, Keyshawn, where you at!"

"What chu need?" the man responded, peeping around the outside corner of the building.

"It's a customer waitin' on you, what chu think!"

"Awh, my bad," Keyshawn said, strangling one last draw on a cigarette he'd just lit. He exhaled the toxins and stepped the ignited ashes into the ground. Strolling, as though people came to here just to see him walk, he eventually made his way to Randall's car. He had hair that was either terribly styled or horribly combed. Whatever that case, Randall found it unappealing and nowhere close to professional.

"'S'happenin'?" he murmured, exposing gold-covered teeth. He looked like he'd just eaten gold-plated chocolate or perhaps brushed his teeth with gold-plated toothpaste.

"I'm fine, how you doin'?" Randall replied, offended.

"Um aihgt. What chu need?"

Randall was puzzled. "What do you mean what I need? Ain't this an oil change place? What else would I get here?"

"I'm just sayin'," Keyshawn said, pulling up his pants that where running down his butt, racing for his ankles. "You coulda had wanted a transmission service or somethin', shawty."

"No. What I want is a oil change. That's what I been wantin' for the last five minutes I been out here waitin' for you to finish yo' cigarette."

"My bad," he replied scratching his chin showing his darkened fingertips and nails. The lips covering his shiny gold teeth were dull blue. He had all the telltale signs of a weed smoker's makeover.

"Need to get some info from you," he said, pulling a pad from his pocket and a pencil from deep within the confines of his hair. You been here before."

Randall wasn't sure if he was asking or telling.

"No."

"Last name."

"Harvey."

"How you spell dat?"

Randall rattled off the spelling and waited for the next question. The man looked baffled.

"H-A- what?" Keyshawn asked. Randall looked at him, frustrated. He was growing more agitated every second.

Randall dashed through the letters the man was missing.

"R-V-E what?"

"Y!" Randall yelled. He spelled the name again this time slowly and condescending. "H – A – R – V – E – Y. You got it?"

"Yeah, I feel ya," he replied not realizing he'd been slighted. "Yearuh."

"Huh?" Randall asked.

"Yearuh."

"What the hell is a Yee-ra?"

"The Yearuh yo' cah was made. What else?"

"Is that what you said? Year!"

"Yeah. What Yearuh is it?"

"Young man," Randall said, reaching through the window. "Let me fill this thing out myself because I ain't got enough time to figure out what language you speakin' or why some teacher let you outta high school."

"Yeah, whateva, man. Pull on in the bay. I'm gon' show you in."

Randall waited for the gold-toothed scarecrow to walk ahead of his car and give directions. Keyshawn looked at Randall's front tires, checking the alignment of his wheels with the proper position of the oil change bay path. He fanned his right hand toward his own chest telling Randall to pull forward. His left hand continued fighting the falling pants that had never seen a belt. He pointed his thumb to the left and right, bringing the car to the guides in order for the technician underneath to begin the procedure. Finally, Keyshawn held his hand palm out to Randall, stopping the car.

"Place yo' cah in pahk gon' inside be witchu lata."

"Huh? Never mind," Randall said, exiting the car and waiting in the small room equipped with a television, coffee maker, and soda machine. The man who'd yelled for Keyshawn sat behind a counter focused only on a Jerry Springer episode filled with bleeps and body parts covered by blurry censored patches all over the screen.

This is pitiful, Randall thought to himself. *How they gon' run a business treatin' people like...* He paused in his own frustration as a transformation took place. His mind began tearing down the walls of this building. The Jerry Springer fan and Keyshawn vanished. New walls sprang up around him, walls that were familiar in size, color, and location. Randall blinked, thinking it was a fainting spell. Maybe the grief and agony of losing his child, coupled with business

stresses, had overtaken him. The shop had been transformed into his own restaurant.

Only he wasn't working there. Instead, he was his
own customer. Veronica, adorned in her typical deco-
rative ghetto gown, was at the register. Randall stood
there, waiting for her to greet him, take his order,
anything. She just stood in front of him, taking long,
exaggerated drags on her death stick. He kept waiting
as he heard the Culture Complex jingle over the
speaker system in his own restaurant. Veronica continued to smoke as if he weren't there. Finally, she
spoke. "You ready, shawty?" Even her voice had
taken on a transformation. In this daydream where
everything was foreign but familiar, his daughter
sounded exactly like Keyshawn. "Hey, what chu gon'
do? Come on now. I ain't got all day."

Randall wanted so badly to tell his daughter she
couldn't greet people that way. That she had to be
cordial and fast. That she had to be articulate, look
professional. But he couldn't form the words. He
could only hear her say in the rambled voice of Keyshawn, "Hey, you ready? What chu gon' do? Come
on now, I need to check you out. Yo' cah ready."

Then there was a shove on his shoulder, waking
him from the trance. The building came back, as did
the Springer fan and Keyshawn standing in front of
him, tugging at his deflated pants and saying the
words he'd just heard Veronica utter. Randall looked
at him, wondering what had just happened, what the
vision meant. Keyshawn babbled more gibberish that

may or may not have meant he'd completed the job. Randall paid the Springer fanatic, who was still looking at the screen while counting bills and dispensing change. He gave Randall a receipt, never once looking at him. Randall dashed out the door, into his car, and off to the other side of the tracks.

Randall made his way to Interstate 285 still thinking of his vision. His eyes were looking at the road but he saw the images again. Veronica and Keyshawn. Himself as an unsatisfied patron. He traveled on a bit further and noticed an orange illumination coming from his instrument panel. A small picture of an oil can beamed the bright message that something was wrong. Randall cursed the light, hoping it would go away after a few thumps on the plastic face covering the panel. All of his money was drowning in the business and he had very little to repair his car—none if this light meant mechanical doom.

Back came the memories of Daniel Lee's conversation about Hispanics piled in one car and one car note for ten people as opposed to every one of *your people* having their own car note. His car had been performing oddly and he hoped the oil change would help, but now he thought it had become worse. Maybe Keyshawn had gremlined it.

He pulled off at the Pleasant Hill Road exit, just minutes away from Corey. There he saw another branch of the same oil change franchise he'd just left. He quickly pulled around to the back. Before he'd even had a chance to roll his window down, a clean-shaven young man with sandy brown hair and freckles to match sprinted to the driver's side of Randall's car.

"Hello, sir! Welcome to Jiffy Lube. Do you need an oil change today?"

Randall was pleasantly startled. "Well, actually I just had an oil change at yo' other store."

The boy's face changed from excitement to disappointment, the way a child looks when the promise of playing catch or riding a bike is suddenly unfulfilled.

"Sir, was there a problem?"

"Well, I'm not sure. My check oil light just came on and —"

"Sir, pull it in here. We'll take a look at it for you right away. David! Pull in on two, please."

Another man appeared, wearing his uniform pressed and as clean as a oil-change uniform could be. A matching cap neatly held back his red hair. He ran to the front of the oil bay and directed Randall in with the care and precision of a ground crew bringing in a jet. Quickly, he disappeared and Randall felt the man pushing and pulling underneath the car before he could even grab for the handle to open the door. The freckled man opened Randall's door and said, "Sir, if you'd like you can have a seat in our comfortable waiting room. We'll come and get you as soon as we know something."

"Thank you," Randall said, still amazed at the service. "Here's my receipt if you —"

"No need, sir. I already saw the sticker on your window and I noticed the date. You're fine."

Randall walked towards the waiting room while the man opened the hood of Randall's car.

"I got it!" the man under the hood yelled down to the man below. "It's up top, David. No oil cap."

Randall heard the conversation and headed back to the car.

"What happened?" asked Randall.

"Sir, it looks like they forgot to put your oil cap back on. You've lost a few quarts of oil. Has your oil light ever come on before?"

"Nawh. Not that I know of."

"That should be it, then."

"Damn, now I gotta go buy a oil cap and then—"

"No sir, we've got a cap for this model. Let me fill her back up with oil and I'll put a new one on for you."

"And how much is that gon' cost? Y'all's parts is higher than the store, I know."

"No charge, sir. We'll square it away with the other store. I apologize for your inconvenience."

Randall was stunned, amazed, and then shocked at the entire experience. The fast service, the professional appearance of the workers, the courtesy. It was all rather frightening. There was no vision of his own business here, no sign of his daughter's counterpart. He realized that this was how he wanted to be treated as a customer, and suddenly he began thinking it might be too late.

Randall was jarred from his thoughts by the sound of his hood closing. The man who'd been quick to bring him in was escorting him out with the same pleasantries. Randall hopped in and drove off. Now *he* had something to talk to his son about.

There was a McDonald's near the onramp of the interstate. It reminded him that he'd promised to pick up something for Corey. Randall looked at the clock and discovered that nearly an hour had passed since he told Corey he'd be right over. He sped to the drive thru, noticing the nice landscaping surrounding the order menu.

Purples and yellows contrasted with each other while reds and oranges blended together to form a horticultural rainbow. Pine straw was neatly spread over the areas that outlined freshly cut, lush green Bermuda grass. The more appetizing meals were prominently displayed on the board, enticing customers to pick the high-ticket items. Just as Randall came to a halt, a kind voice floated through the speaker.

"Welcome to McDonald's. Would you like to try one of our combo meals today?"

Randall picked up the accent. It was similar to the one he'd heard from Juan Santos.

"Yeah let me get a uhhh…a uhhh. A number five and a number two."

"Okay. Sir. That's a Big Mac combo meal and a double cheeseburger combo meal. Would you like to upsize those today? You get a free apple pie with up-

size meal." The woman's voice was upbeat and energetic. Randall almost felt guilty thinking of not taking
her up on the offer.

"Yeah, go ahead and upsize 'em."

"Great. Jour total is eight eighty-nine. Please drive
around to de first window."

Randall released his brake and coasted up to a
window marked with a large red number one. He
was rolling, reaching for his wallet, when the face attached to the voice leaned out the window to greet
him. The drive-thru headset rested neatly on her
cropped black hair. She smiled at Randall, gleaming
white teeth against her golden bronze skin. A tiny
black mole sat just off the side of her upper lip, which
had been gently grazed by a complimenting hue of
lipstick. She was pleasant to look at, Randall thought
to himself. Made him feel good about eating here.

"Hello. How are you today? Eight eighty-nine
please."

"Here you go," Randall said, returning her smile
and placing a ten-dollar bill in her hand.

"Thank you and here's jour change," she said
without reaching for the register. She'd already anticipated that the customer would pay with a ten or
two fives and had change ready for a fast exchange
"Please pull to next window. Hab a nice day."

Randall nodded and waved, feeling obligated to
respond to the woman's kind ways. He tossed the
change into his ashtray and coasted up to the next
window where he saw a young man with the same

smile and skin tone as the woman from window one. Just as Randall stopped, the man was holding a large bag out of the window filled with the contents of Randall's order.

"Thank you. Hab nice day," the man said, struggling a bit with the language and his confidence. A lady in a manager's uniform spoke with him, pointing to different areas in the drive-thru bay. As the window began to close, Randall could hear fluent Spanish flowing through the small area and realized that man was undergoing intense training.

Randall's stomach began to rumble with hunger and fear—he could clearly see that this was a well-run business. And his was not. He pulled toward the exit and reached in the bag to ease part of the pain with a french fry. As he poked around in the bag, he realized that something was missing. He slammed the brakes and threw the car in reverse, backing into a parking space. Randall jumped from the car and entered the restaurant.

At the scene inside, the grumbling in his stomach worsened immediately. The store was filled with people. People moving, people eating, people smiling, people giving money. Randall looked behind the counter and every face he saw was hustling, every face he saw was communicating with another, every face he saw behind a cash register was smiling, and every face he saw in an employee uniform—was bronze.

A bronze man was mopping the floor of the already immaculately clean lobby. Despite the restaurant being filled with people, the condiment table was clean and orderly. Trash cans were neat and sanitized. Randall watched as a soda fell to the floor, its liquids flowing underneath a table. The mopping man dipped his wet tool into the bucket, wrung out the excess water, and sped over to the area. He cleaned the mess so quickly, the man seemed to have reversed time in a matter of seconds. Then off he darted back behind the counter. He ran back with a fresh cup of the soda that had been spilled, gave it to the customer, and continued his mopping.

"Sir, did you just come through drive thru?" a bronze woman asked warmly. She was the manager Randall had seen in the window. He was so entranced at how the employees were working he didn't see her approach.

"Huh? Oh yeah. I did. Wasn't I suppose to get free pies if I upgraded my meal?"

"Oh yes, sir. You didn't get them? I am sorry about that." She yelled back to an employee, "¡No se te puede dividar dareles un pasteles con las orderes extra grandes!"

The woman dashed away just as the mop man had. She came back seconds later with the missing parts of Randall's meal. "Here you are, sir. Be careful because they are very hot. And I'm sorry you had to come back. Here's a coupon for a free combo meal during your next visit. Come back and see us soon."

Randall, with hot food in one hand and extreme customer satisfaction in the other, drove off in his car and instantly saw another vision of his own restaurant. This time he was standing outside, looking in during the lunch time rush. He saw a large sign in the window that simply read...GONE OUT OF BUSINESS.

Chapter Nineteen

Reconciliation

Randall arrived at the gas station where Corey had been waiting. The station had a small Subway restaurant like many of the more modern gas stops did. People were pumping gas, shopping, and eating all at the same place these days. Business owners saw the potential of expanding their market and were beginning to take full advantage of it.

Corey was sitting at one of the two booths for patrons who chose to dine in at a gas station or perhaps rest from a long stretch of driving. When Randall pulled up, Corey headed outside and ignored the Indian cashier wishing him a good day as he walked out.

"Pops, thanks for comin' to get me. I thought you got lost for a minute."

"Nawh. I was dealin' with some ol' trifflin' Negroes down in Decatur. I don't know how some people stay in business. You ready to go? I brought you somethin' to eat."

"Yeah, let's head out," he replied, getting into Randall's car as they drove off.

"What you gon' do about the car?"

"Uh, I guess it'll stay there until I get some money to fix it. I think the alternator went bad."

"You can't leave the car on the road like that. Somebody'll break into it or they'll tow it."

Corey looked at his father with eyes of young revelation, finding out one of life's facts often discovered only through misfortune.

"How long you think it'll be before somebody tows it?" Corey asked.

"Why you just won't tow it yourself?"

Corey looked out of the window and answered, "I ain't got no extra money. In fact I ain't got no money at all."

"Say what?" What you doin' with all yo' money? Ain't you workin' two jobs? You can't afford a tow for your car?"

"I'm tryin' to save some money, so I can move."

"Huh? Move where? Where you goin?"

"I was thinkin' about goin' to Texas and tryin' to get a job on a oil rig or somethin' like that. Saw a website for this company called Coleman Rigs."

"What! Who the hell you know in Texas and what
you know about a oil rig? Corey, why you wanna…"
Randall stopped his machine gun questioning and
found his answer in the young man's solemn stare.
His brother was gone, his father's business was failing, and the already strained family was falling apart.
Randall thought about the period of time since his
son's death. He wondered if there had been enough
grieving, enough tears shed. Had there been enough
emotional releases? Anger had smothered the family's sadness and Randall still hadn't spoken to Veronica about her feelings. Didn't ask how she was
doing, what would make it better, what would ease
her pain. Randall hadn't cried in front of what was
left of his family. He'd been their fearless leader but
he realized there had been some failure in leading
them through this time. As he suppressed his own
feelings by shoving more distractions into the pres-
sure-packed pipe of his life, Randall carried on as
though he'd reached resolution for his son's death.
He suspected, however, that Corey had not.

"It's hard for you, ain't it?" Randall said.

"What, workin' two jobs?"

"Nawh, I mean…losin' yo' brother."

Corey whipped around to face his father when he
mentioned the lost sibling. The thought upset him.

"Why you say that?" he responded defensively.

"'Cause all of sudden you talkin' about leavin' and
you not thinkin' straight. It's because of yo' brother,
ain't it? I know I probably ain't helped y'all with that

as much as I should have, but you know everybody got they own way of dealin' wit' it you know? Veronica havin' problems too, I know it. I just don't know what to say to her. All I wanna do is provide for y'all and kill whoever took my boy. I swear to God I though it was them Mexicans."

"What you mean you *thought* it was?"

"That heifer Karen Batch swear up and down they didn't do it and —"

"What does she know?"

"Don't ask me. But somehow she say they didn't do it and it was sabotage or somethin'. Then come to find out, the police supposed to have a good lead on who did it."

"How you know that?"

"One of the detectives, Chris Askew, calls me every week givin' updates. I guess he feel obligated. He left me a message — somethin' about a video tape they got from Santos's place."

"A video! Where the video been all this time! How come they ain't said nothin' until now? Pops, those Mexicans is lyin'!"

"Why you think so?"

"How they all of sudden get a video tape? Why they ain't tell nobody about it when Santos was in front of the camera talkin' about how his restaurant is so clean? I'm tellin' you, they lyin'!"

"So, you think they just made a fake videotape of somebody breakin' in?"

"How should I know?" Corey was livid. "All I know is you need to go talk to Santos and find out what he know. Find out why he wait so long to send in a videotape. You wanna make me feel better, find out why them Mexicans lyin' about killin' my brother. This oughta make the police look at them closer now. It just don't make no sense. You see what I'm sayin'?"

Randall searched the road ahead, looking for answers, trying to stumble upon on the right thing to say.

"I guess so. Never thought about it that way. Now you mention it, it do seem a little odd that they didn't say nothin' about the tape earlier. I hate to call that cop back and he feed me somethin' like they'll look into it. I don't know if Santos'll even see me and I'm not sure I wanna see him. Besides, I might throw my hands around his neck if I get close enough anyway."

"Pops, you need to talk to him. You need to talk to him quick."

"Who, the cop?"

"Nawh, that lyin' Santos! Find out what he know," Corey said, turning away once again, the road racing by. "Here's my car up ahead. You think I could borrow some money for a tow?" Randall was thinking through the events, playing scenarios in his mind. "Pops!"

"Huh?"

"The tow, remember? I'm gon' need to borrow some money."

"Oh yeah, son. No problem. I'll do whatever I can to help."

"Juan, someone is here to see you," a young lady announced.

"Who is it?"

"It's me," Randall said, barging past the lady and into Juan's office.

He'd taken his son's advice and decided to visit Santos. Most of the night was spent thinking of questions to ask. The other parts of the night were spent thinking of ways to react violently in case there was an opportunity. He'd even spent a little time thinking of punches to throw and ways to fight dirty, in case it came down to that. Randall thought of bringing his gun so that he might be prepared if there was another showdown.

Juan pushed back from his desk at the sound of Randall's voice. His face was tinting a light shade of red and his hand was slowly heading for the bottom drawer where his gun was waiting.

"Sorry to come by unannounced but there's something I wanna ask you about," Randall said to a motionless Juan. "First, I guess I need to apologize for what happened at the hospital. People just act without thinking in a time like that. Guess there really ain't no right way to react when somethin' like that happen. So, I'm sorry for what happened out there that day." Randall left the apology hanging, waiting, hoping that Juan would pick it up and respond. There was nothing, although Juan's hand stopped moving towards the drawer.

"Also, I guess I need to congratulate you on the grant. I heard that y'all won it. Amazin' considerin' everything y'all been through." This time Juan tilted his head slightly and squinted. "Mind if I sit down?" Again, Juan offered him nothing. "Look, man. What you want me to say? This been a real bad time in my life and all I wanna do is ask you some questions. When I learn how to deal it, I'm gon' need to know everything I can about what happened to my boy. I'm tryin' to make things right for everybody. You lucky 'cause you ain't got to worry about how yo' business is…You know what? I don't even know why I came by here. Shoulda known you didn't want to help me with no questions."

Randall walked to the door, thinking of the punches he was practicing the night before. Three swift stingers and he could have left Juan unconscious in no time. Then he remembered how quick Juan had pulled the gun. As Randall turned the doorknob, Juan said, "Why don't you ask de police your questions?"

"I already talked to the police. Talked to 'em more than once, as a matter of fact."

"Then why are you here?"

"'Cause you supposed to have a tape or somethin' ain't you?"

"I do not have tape. Someone else has tape or maybe police have it now."

"There's a tape, but you don't know where it is?"

"No."

Randall smirked. He began to recall some of the questions he'd prepared so that he could catch Juan in a lie. As he walked away from the door and headed for Juan, he was stopped by Juan's hand once again heading for the drawer. The cold stillness returned to Juan's face.

"Why all of a sudden you got a tape, but you didn't have one when you was talkin' on TV?"

"I did not know about it."

"So, how you find out about it, now."

"Someone bring to me."

"Who?"

"My employee."

"Who?"

"Why?" Juan asked, continuing his short, cold answers.

"'Cause I wanna know, that's why!" Randall exclaimed, causing Juan to revert back to his initial demeanor, calm and quiet. "Who gave you the tape?"

Juan sat back in his seat, his face stretched with a look of scorn.

"What's his name or her name?" Randall asked, not yet realizing that this was a game. A game that Juan was controlling—give Juan respect, Juan gives answers.

179

"Where they get a tape from? Did they make the tape?" Randall was a bad business owner but an even worse detective. Frustrated, he waved his hand at Juan, and headed for the door when he remembered that it was the submission that Juan initially responded to. It was then that he quickly learned the game.

"Okay, I was wrong for yellin' like that. I'm sorry again. If you could just tell me when your employee found the tape, I'd appreciate it."

"Before your son died." Juan said, wishing he'd known a more gentle way to say it. "I'm sorry for your loss," he added.

"You got a video camera around here."

"It was new camera. I did not know."

"Did you see the tape?"

"Jes."

"You recognize the person that did it?"

"Jes."

"You tell the police?"

"No."

"Why not?"

"Why is important to you?"

Randall felt another outburst coming on, but then remembered how much easier it was to speak with humility. After a long, deep sigh, he replied, "I just wonder if you saw the tape and you know who did it, why you ain't told the cops. It makes me wonder if there really is a tape. And if there is a tape, is it for real. I mean, is it a fake?"

"Why?"

"Why what?" asked Randall.

"Why is tape important to ju?"

"My son is gone and somebody need to get gone too. Just seems like if you had the information you would have gave it to the police by now."

"That is what you want?"

"I want some damn justice is what I want!"

Juan froze up again, but this time in his own epiphany. He now realized Randall had no way of knowing and could not have been involved.

Juan paused for a moment, struggling with responses. "You believe in justice?"

"Damn right. And whoever killed my boy need to get some of it."

Juan straightened papers on his desk and closed the bottom drawers, hoping there would be no need to use his weapon.

"Justice can be a tragedy. That is why I have no give to police. I give tape to someone who know about the people in tape and I tell him. Make it right. Maybe he give to police, maybe he give justice for he self. But I cannot give to police myself. I know of justice and it not always best."

"Hold on, wait a minute. You tryin' to tell me you know who did this and you ain't doin' nothin' about it?"

"No. I doing something about it, but it my justice."

"That don't make no sense. Somebody got to go to jail for this," Randall said as he watched Juan rise empty-handed from his desk. "Why wouldn't you just give to the...what kinda justice you talkin' about...At least tell me this..."

Randall was slowly becoming exhausted. Although so much had been revealed, he still knew nothing. Randall could sense the honesty in Juan and his plan of attack had become one of surrender. "Did somebody do this on purpose or was it an accident? You know, like somebody not washin' they hands after they came back from usin' the bathroom. How you know somebody that work here just didn't make a mistake?"

"I show you. Come to back door, you see. On the, eh, tape they left de building when it was closed-ed. It no mistake. They meant to hurt people."

Chapter Twenty

Mergers & Accusations

Juan escorted Randall through the restaurant as the busy staff carried out their tasks. It reminded Randall of the hustle he'd seen at the well-run McDonald's. Yet this was behind the scenes.

The kitchen was sanitized and clean. A germ couldn't survive for more than an hour before it was wiped away or disinfected. Despite Randall's attempts over the years, he was never able to keep his kitchen clean for an entire shift and by day's end, he always had a cleaning disaster on his hands.

"Gabriel, don't forget to check the bathrooms again. Little boy run in there twenty minutes ago," Juan said to a man already consumed with sweeping the floor.

"Si." Juan stopped his authoritative march at the sound of the man's voice. Randall bumped into him, unable to anticipate the abrupt halt. "Yes, sir," the sweeping man said, correcting himself. Juan continued on as Randall kept gawking at the pace and efficiency of Juan's employees.

"It back here near the door," Juan said to no one. Randall was still ten feet behind Juan, watching the machine of energetic people conduct business of the day. "Mr. Harby...Mr. Harby."

"Huh?"

"It back here."

"Oh...yeah. Uh, where did you get these people? They all related to you?"

Juan was flattered, while at the same time surprised that this was something Randall had never seen.

"Jes, some of them are related, but we are all familia. I am sure you have this type of hard workers at your place."

"Well...uh...yeah. I got people that bust they tail all day for me," he lied. "But how you get all of 'em to work like this? Look like they dancin'."

A lady whizzed by the two and tossed a bag of lettuce to a man standing over a grill. The man whipped out a knife, stabbed the plastic bag and watched the lettuce fall into a stainless steel container. The man was whistling, watching the order screen, and flipping food on the sizzling surface. A young man darted back and forth from cash registers, filling orders with lightning speed. Each tray was delivered with a smile before he hurried off to the next order.

"I did not make them work like this. I just hire them and they are hungry enough to work this way. Before I hire, I talk to each of them. I ask where they from, what was it like for them in Mexico. And I only hire the one that were hungry and the one that have hard time in Mexico, 'cause I know they are good people. Good people come from bad times and they want to do better. They will work hard for it.

"La Familia is nothing without it people. I have the best people I can find here. They work hard and I pay them very good. When they work hard we have good business. Good business bring us more customer and more customer bring us more money to pay good people. I think you have same good people at your place, no?"

"No. I mean, yeah," Randall lied again, still watching the people flow through the building. He thought about his own restaurant at busy times. It was discombobulated at best. No one rushed, no one worked together unless they were yelling at each other in frustration. And even then, tasks were completed to shut the other person up. He thought about his own hiring process. A person would fill out a job application. Randall would call people for interviews based on what hours the applicant could work as opposed to their experience. Then he would hire based on when they could begin instead of how they felt about working. Suddenly he thought of his daughter, the worst employee he had. He could never find the courage to let her go, no matter how much she hurt the business.

"I want to show this and then I have to go over to Culture Complex. We are selling our quesadillas recipe to them," Juan said heading for the back door. "Have you seen Complex yet?"

"Yeah I seen that mess. Don't know why you sellin' a recipe to them. Ain't gon' last more than a year."

"I think it will last for long time. But if it does not, we will still have the money they gave to buy our formula."

"And how much is that?"

"I cannot discuss. I promise Mr. Lee. But if they stay open more than three years, they will pay us enough to buy more equipment."

"What! They givin' you that much money for a recipe?"

"Not just recipe. Also license to use. Very generous offer."

"Damn."

"Here is camera," Juan said as they both stepped out the back door. The two looked up and saw a tiny hole no one would notice unless they knew exactly where to look.

"How long you had that up there?" asked Randall.

"A week before people get sick. New employee put it in. People seem to do things all the time to make La Familia better without telling me."

"So you had no idea this was up here?"

"Not until they say."

"You sure it was before my boy got sick?"

"I don't think my people lie to me. No one want to hurt La Familia except man I saw in video. I know his family in Mexico. That why I not go to police."

"That don't make no damn sense. Is he still here? He work for you? If this is the man that killed my boy, then the police got to know. You hear me! That's my justice!"

Juan stepped back from the angered Randall and regretted that he had not brought his weapon. He looked at Randall, holding firm to what little courage his eyes would show. Finally, Randall was remorseful for his eruption.

"Santos, I'm sorry. Just a little wound up right now. Well…tell me…I mean what would you do if it was yo' boy?"

"I want justice too."

"Exactly! So why you ain't told the police? I need to know who did this thing."

"I say justice, not punish. Sometime police not give justice, they punish. Justice send man back to Mexico and make him live the way we used to. I make him decide what to do with tape to make it right. He never want to go back to Mexico, so he will do right thing."

"My boy dead. The right thing gotta be just as bad or it's gonna be worse when I find 'em. Unless yo'

man gon' kill hisself or kill that other fool, he bedda hope the police get the tape.

"That not justice, that punishment. He will do the right thing. I know his family. People will know who did and you will know what justice is. You not like it when you see it. I am afraid. He will give to police or he will find the other man and make him go to the police. That justice. When a man must make hisself do the right thing."

The two stood out back, watching delivery trucks pass by and the world move on to its next emergency.

"I am sure police will find out about the other man. You should talk to them. I must go now," Juan said, ending the conversation. If they continued, Juan would be compelled to reveal all that he knew.

"Huh?" Randall said, still drowning in Juan's wisdom and civility "Oh yeah, okay. Appreciate cha." He extended his hand to Juan, perhaps their first and only merger.

"Karen—I mean...uh, Mrs. Batch—. I think I need to apologize for some of the things I been sayin' to you over the last few months. I done seen some things that back up what you been sayin' about business."

"Really?" Karen said, surprised Randall's call was of a civil nature. She'd been waiting for a surprise attack, maybe from the bushes or a crazed car chase on the interstate. However, she had not at all anticipated a peace offering. Security had been notified after their last phone fight and until now, Randall hadn't tried to contact her office. "This is quite a surprise, Mr. Harvey. Our last conversation ended rather abruptly so you'll forgive me if I'm taken aback."

"And that's really one of the reasons that I called. Guess I was out of line on that right there, so I gotta say I'm sorry 'bout that. Just been so many things goin' on right now—"

"I can certainly understand that, Mr. Harvey. Anyone in your current state has the right to have some frustrations."

"Appreciate that, Mrs. Batch. It's just, you know my boy is gone, I ain't really talked to my daughter about it, and when we didn't get that grant, it was all I could do to not kill nobody. Now, I ain't sayin' I wanted to kill you or nothin' like that."

The prickly sensation of fear crawling up Karen's back quickly subsided.

"But that day everything came down at one time and I ain't know how to deal with it. You just happened to be there when I blew up and that wasn't right."

"That's very noble of you, Mr. Harvey. Thank you for saying that. What was the other thing?"

"Huh?"

"You said that was one of the things you called about. What was the other?"

"Oh, that's right. I almost forgot. I need your help with somethin'. Lately, I been seein' and noticing some things that's got me thinkin' about my restaurant and how I been doin' business. I think it's about time that I change the way we run our place. You know, I really want to be in good shape when that grant come around next year. And if I'm gon' do that, I guess I need some help. Some real help. Somebody to come in and look at my books, take a look at how we get folks in and out, look at the way I hire people, look at how much we charge, how the place is decorated. You know, just anything that could make us better."

"That's great news, Mr. Harvey. This is exactly what we had in mind when we started the project. The better businesses would be recognized and other businesses would learn from ones like Mr. Santos'. This is all very commendable of you."

"Now, I ain't gon' lie to ya. It hurt like hell when you told me Santos had done won. But hey, y'all was in charge and y'all gave it to who y'all thought was the best. Next year…it's gon' be another story. And that's why I'm callin'. I need yo' help gettin' my business back off the ground. Don't need no money or nothin' like that—well I do, but that's another phone call. Just want yo' office to help out showin' us how to do better. Don't y'all do consultin' and stuff like that? How much somethin' like that costs?"

"We do and we don't. We used to, anyway. I'm afraid to say that we're closing our office."

"What! Why come?"

"My husband got on offer in Telaquah, Oklahoma for a long term construction contract. It's a once-in-a-lifetime opportunity and it will give his company a chance to really make a name for itself in his industry. So, we're leaving very soon and the office is closing. I'm sorry."

"Damn." Randall was silent. It seemed as though each time he called or visited this place there was never a pleasant outcome. His restaurant was closed, he was ready to make necessary changes for improvement, but now the help he'd already counted on was moving away. "What's gon' happen to the grant thing?"

"For this year, it won't change. Mr. Santos will receive all of the funding, but next year, there may not be an award unless someone comes along and orchestrates the project. We've been talking to a few non-profit organizations, but so far there are no real definite leads. I'm sorry. We would have loved to have worked with you and helped your business grow. You should try the small business center. They can help with reshaping your business."

"They ain't gon' have no grant though, are they?"

"Mmm, probably not, but it's not always about what you can get in return for something," Karen said, placing desk items in a box. She'd begun packing for the move the day after her husband had told her about the project in Oklahoma. "Sometimes we need to do things because they need to be done. Because those things will make us better, make our business better."

"I can think of a whole lotta ways to make my business better with a million dollars."

"And the small business center can think of several ways to improve your business with little or no money. You really should give them a call. Is there anything else I can help you with? Don't mean to rush you, but we're on a tight schedule — selling the house, finding a new one, packing. That kinda thing."

Randall sighed, feeling dejected after acting on his epiphany. "Nawh, I guess that's all I had to ask. Suppose I oughta thank you for doin' what you did anyway. Maybe it'll help more businesses than we know."

"You're quite welcome. Don't beat yourself up too bad. After all, you did make it to the final round of evaluations and that shows the potential of your establishment. One good mystery shopper score and you were right there. Keep in touch with us. I'd love to hear how things turn out for you. You're a strong-willed man, Mr. Harvey, just like my father. And thanks for calling. Take care."

"Okay, you do the—" Randall tried to rush his words before the inevitable click pounced in his ear. He hung up the phone, her words still ringing in his conscience. Potential. Improvement. Strong-willed. It was a different tone than she'd ever communicated before. No longer were they business people, or even adversaries. The compliment she'd given rang true of a conversation he hadn't had in quite some time. A conversation he should have had long before now. It was time to talk to his daughter before he completely lost her.

Chapter Twenty-One

Daddy's Big Girl

Randall found his daughter on what he thought was the verge of an emotional breakdown. She was pacing the floor and shaking. She yelled at Randall as he walked through the door of her apartment.

"Daddy, where my brother at?"

"Huh? Babygirl, you know we lost Jessie. What's wrong with you?"

"No, Daddy. I can't find Corey either. Why y'all keep leavin' me!"

"Veronica. Calm down. Corey work all the time lately. We right here, baby. Ain't nobody gon' leave you."

"Stop lyin' to me! Y'all tryin' to leave me, ain't you? Jessie gone, Corey leavin' just like mama left.

Why the hell y'all keep runnin' from me? What's wrong wit' me! Why people be hatin' me, Daddy!"

"Baby, baby. Don't say that. We not leavin' you. Come here, Veronica." Randall reached for his irate daughter and pulled her close, trying to bury her concern in his chest.

He'd forgotten the role of comforting father soon after he'd started the restaurant years ago. Merely a dream at its inception, the establishment swallowed his time and slowly consumed his life. Randall never trusted people to operate his business. He never hired anyone to help out so that he might get some much-needed rest and spend the desperately needed time with his family. His solution was to hire his children into the business, hoping that one day they would own the corporation, selling franchises around the country. Hiring his three blessings was an opportunity to spend time with them. Nurture their lives and watch them blossom, or so he thought. Randall never realized that Jessie was the only child who truly enjoyed working for him. He arrived for work early, completed tasks beyond his responsibility, and stayed as late as Randall allowed. Jessie saw the potential of his father's business and eagerly awaited the day that Randall would make him manager.

Corey simply saw the restaurant as a paycheck until one of his other ventures proved successful. He showed up for work when he wanted and rarely did more than was needed of him, many times barely doing what was asked. He never wanted to put in the selfless work, but yearned for the selfish greed.

Veronica loathed the business. She despised the meager wages and detested each customer who walked through the door. Most of all, she resented the time her father spent away from her. While other girls were working through growing pains with their parents, Veronica was simply working—at a greasy fish shack. She felt as though this place had taken her life, just as it had taken her brother's life. Here she lay now, sobbing, resting in what had become a foreign place—her father's arms.

"What's wrong wit' me?" she asked.

"Huh? Why you say that?" Randall asked, pushing her a short distance away so he could look at her face and search for answers. "What makes you think somethin' wrong wit' chu?"

"Daddy, I called Corey nine times and he ain't called me back. You don't never want to talk to me unless I'm at work. And since you done closed the place to get remodeled, I ain't workin' at all. Is that why you don't talk to me now?"

"Veronica, you a grown woman. I ain't think you needed ya old man that much no more. I know we ain't talked much about Jessie, but I thought that was yo' way of dealin' wit' things."

"How do I deal wit' things, Daddy? Matter of fact, how do I do anything?" Veronica asked, backing away from Randall. "Do you even know how I do anything except work a cash register? Do you know

what my favorite color is? You know who my boy-
friend is? Do you know me at all? Do you know how
many times I been pregnant?"

"What?" Randall exclaimed. He was horrified,
both at his own negligence and the thought of un-
known secrets.

"Mm-hmm. That's what I thought. You don't want
me around here either, do you? 'Cause if you did, you
would know my life. We live in the same damn city,
work at the same place, and all you know is my
name."

"What the hell you talkin' about, bein' pregnant? I
know you ain't out there havin' sex. Now, I done told
you that ain't my department. You need to watch
yo'self out there 'cause I can't help with all that stuff."

Veronica looked at her father, dumbfounded. She
chuckled.

"I don't see nothin' funny!"

"You funny. Whenever I need somethin' for me—
and I don't mean some clothes or nothin' like that—
but when I need you to teach me about life, or about
men, it ain't never yo' department. Right before Jessie
got sick, what was you doin'?"

Randall looked at the floor, outside the window,
then back at Veronica, but never found the answer. "I
don't know, it was so much goin' on at—"

"You was tryin' to teach me how to be nice to
them old nasty customers that come up in there all
the time. And that's what I'm talkin' about. You always got time to show me how to work and you can

always talk to me about what I gotta do to make the restaurant better, but you can't never tell me how to make *me* better. You ain't never done that. Daddy, I ain't never been pregnant, ever. You know why, 'cause I always protect myself when I'm—"

"Whoa, whoa! Babygirl, I *don't* need to hear—"

"You gon' hear it, today. And you gon' hear it good. I use protection and you know how I know to use protection? 'Cause Corey told me to. And how did he know? 'Cause you told him to."

Randall stood, stupefied, numbed by his daughter's cold glare and the frightening revelations she was unveiling.

"But you never told me about sex, you never told me about all the stuff you told him. How you think I made it this far? Did you know me and Corey used to have Daddy talks? He used to come in my room and tell me all the stuff you taught him. That's how I learned what I had to know, from what you taught him. And for the longest time, I thought that was how it was supposed to be. The oldest kid would give me and Jessie everything you taught them. I thought that was how it was until Jessie started teachin' me stuff. My own *little brother* was tellin' me stuff I ain't know. Stuff that you had told him. That's how I found out that it was just *me* you wasn't teachin'. You never taught me anything, Daddy."

"That ain't true and you know—"

"I can change a flat. Did you teach me how?"

"Well, I don't—"

"I can cut the grass. You teach me that?"

"What does that have—"

"I can cook. You own a restaurant. You teach me that?"

"Didn't you learn how to—"

"My cycle is irregular sometimes. Did you talk to me about—"

"Hold on, now. I—"

"I get pap smears every—"

"Veronica, that ain't fair," Randall said, fighting the barrage of blame.

"Even if I did get pregnant, how could I know where to get an abor—"

"Veronica, damn it! You stop this! Stop it, right now."

"Why? Why I got to stop? Why I got to do what you say and you never helped me? Why does it matter that—"

"CAUSE SHE SAID SHE WAS COMING RIGHT BACK!" They stared at each other in silence for a moment before Randall exploded with more suppressed anger. "She said she just needed some space! Said she needed the weekend to make things right! She said she was coming right back and when she didn't, I ain't know how to be a mother to a little girl! You know how many damn times I had to go up to that school and get you outta trouble? 'Cause kids picked on you, 'cause you looked funny. Looked funny 'cause I couldn't comb yo' hair the way *she* used to.

199

"You know how many nights I stayed up tryin' to braid that damn doll's hair, just so I could make you look decent enough so kids wouldn't tease you? And no matter what I did, no matter how I tried, I never could make you pretty the way *she* used to. Right then, I knew. I gave up way back then, 'cause I knew I could never be the mother you needed.

"Veronica, I ain't talked to you 'cause I ain't know how. I ain't never knew what to say. I was scared that if I said the wrong thing, it might be that piece of selfishness in you that she had, and you'd leave too. Why you think I gave you that early curfew? I needed you to be home every night 'cause I thought that one day you was gon' tell me you'd be right back." Randall smashed away the salty streams on his face raining down years of repressed feelings.

"She was selfish," he continued, fighting the pain of revelation. "We got married 'cause she wanted a ring before her other friends. We had Corey 'cause she wanted to bring the newest baby to the family reunion. Then, when everybody else had babies, she wanted to be the one with the most babies. We had kids, a house, but she wanted a bigger house, bigger cars. It was always about her. She was so selfish, Veronica. I never knew just how much until Jessie's funeral. I swear I went back to that cemetery and waited until dark. She wasn't at the church so I knew she was gon' come to the cemetery. When she didn't, I thought she was just tryin' to stay out of sight, so I went back and waited for her. She never came. Didn't come to see her own child buried. She was selfish. And I loved her. Even when she walked outta here wit' no clothes, half our money, I loved her enough to believe that she was coming right back. One day I thought she was gon' come back and tell you all these things you need to know. I didn't talk to you 'cause I was too much in love and just stupid enough to think, for years, that she was coming back. I'm sorry."

Randall offered opened arms once again, hoping his daughter would accept his embrace and stay there. Veronica gave her father eyes he'd never seen. Eyes of appreciation. She rushed to her father and fell into his protective arms, being held by the only parent she'd ever had.

"Daddy!" she exclaimed, pulling back and staring at him with fear.

"What's wrong?"

"We gotta find Corey."

"He'll be all right. I told ya, he been workin' all the time lately so he—"

"Nawh, it ain't that. Last time I talked to him, he said the same thing."

"What?"

"He said, 'I'm comin' right back'."

Chapter Twenty-Two

Negotiations

The next day Randall was selling out. He was going to run with whatever he could get and try to salvage what was left of his family. More and more businesses were closing after the Culture Complex continued to dominate by offering more specials, launching more marketing campaigns. Word was spreading through the community about the wonderful services and products the Complex provided. Men were lining up by the dozens to get the five-dollar hair cuts and more women were slowly beginning to make appointments. The Asian stylists duplicated the popular hairstyles in the trendy magazines with no problems. The hair braiders were gaining speed each day, decreasing the time customers had to endure the tedious follicle torture. Empty tables at the restaurant were a rarity, but CLOSED signs at other businesses were abundant.

Randall gave Veronica a new responsibility. Rather than have her deal with customers and hope she wouldn't ruin his business, he gave her the task of selling his business. He'd made a phone call to Daniel Lee that morning, trying his best not to beg, trying to digest the crow he'd had to eat.

"Mr. Lee, this is Randall Harvey."

"Mr. Harvey," he said, waiting for an attack. "How can I help you?" Daniel Lee was less cordial than he'd been at their first meeting.

"A lot been goin' on in my life lately, and I'm tryin' to make things right. I mean, well...I need to say I'm sorry for what I said to you, and I hope that you'll still want to do business wit' me."

Daniel snickered. "Business? Mr. Harvey, in case you haven't noticed, we're doing fine without your recipe. Why would I want to do business with you now?"

"I thought that you seemed like a reasonable man. You makin' all that money and I know you wanna make more. My recipe license could help you do that."

"That may have been the case during our first meeting, but I've had time to grow the business on my own and think about some of the things you said about us. You're out of luck here, Mr. Harvey. Why don't you move your fish shack downtown some-where. They're always looking for failed businesses."

"Why don't you buy the license to my recipe?"

"You didn't hear me the first time? Why would I want to at this point?"

"'Cause you wanna stay in business," Randall re-plied, as the call-waiting signal beeped in his receiver. He ignored the sound and awaited Daniel's response.

"And we will, thank you very much."

"You might."

"Don't start your personal tirade about culturally based businesses again. I'm not in the mood and I have more important matters to take care of."

"Okay, well if you think you'll stay in business long enough to take care of what you got to do then that's fine. But I tried to keep it quiet."

"Keep what quiet?"

"That under-the-table illegal biddin' that I know you and Santos did."

Daniel Lee was quiet for a while. "I...I don't know what you're talking about."

"You ain't got to know. But I know a contractor who bid on yo' job and y'all just about had that whole buildin' done before you even announced who got the job."

"Who told you that?"

"Friend of mine in...uh...Oklahoma."

"Who? You're bluffing. What's their name?"

"They name is Catfish Quesadillas and I don't think you want them to tell everything they know."

"Huh..." Daniel smiled to himself, dropping his head slightly. He'd been checkmated in the scrupulous dealings of business strategy. Tapping his fingers on the desk for a few moments while he deliberated, he continued carefully. "So, Mr. Harvey, what I can do to make this thing work out for both of us."

"Us? Way I see it, all that business you gettin' over there, it's already workin' out for you. I'm the one that need some workin' out for me."

"Just tell me what it is you want. And don't think for one minute we're going to just close up and go away."

"Nawh, nawh. I ain't gon' ask you to do that. I know you got families to take care of and all that. But I got a family too and I ain't been very good to 'em for a long time. I need to get out of this business, Mr. Lee. I figure you can buy the license to my catfish recipe and we'll call it even."

"That's it? That's all you want?"

"It's a big recipe and I expect to get a big price. Understand?"

"Guess it doesn't matter to you that this is blackmail?"

"This? Oh, this ain't blackmail. This is my retirement plan."

"Whatever. What's your price?" Daniel Lee hurried on with frustration.

"Hold on, take your time now. I need help with one more thing. My daughter is gonna come over and negotiate on my behalf. Ain't really no negotiations.

She got a number and if yo' number don't match hers, then I guess we'll negotiate it in the newspapers. Sho' would hate for that to happen, 'cause I done made my peace wit' Santos and he a good man."

"Is that it?"

"That's all. Just treat my baby girl wit' respect. She ain't polished like you. She might not even speak the same English as you. I need you to sit there and treat her like you would some other important person."

"Is that it?" Daniel asked again.

"I think that'll just about do it. She'll be there around three o'clock this afternoon. Her name is Veronica. That's Ms. Veronica Harvey to you."

Randall dialed the code for his voice mail, hoping there would be a response. He'd left several messages for Corey on his cell phone and was waiting for his call. Thoughts of his first child laboring away on an oil rig in the gulf plagued him all night. Had he fallen off the rig? Had there been an accident? Did they have an emergency contact number? There was a message awaiting retrieval. It was the detective calling from a cell phone with a fading signal.

Mr. Harvey. This is Detective Askew… been tryin' to reach you on…business phone. We need you to come over to…. Got a tape from Santos rest…got an arrest warrant out for one…of the…other one…is…deal. The…didn't want

to call you...thought you should come down...need to talk to...Call me...think...you... might need as soon...this message. 404-678-1212...Talk...later.

Randall dialed the number, thinking his timing couldn't have been better. The detective could help him with a missing person report—maybe push through some red tape. He got the detective's voicemail.

"Detective, this is Randall Harvey. Got your message. Look like you got some good news. I'm glad to hear that. Sun startin' to shine on me for a change. I need yo' help wit' somethin'. I ain't been able to get in touch wit' my oldest son. You met him. Corey. I was wondering...well, never mind. I'll head on over there now. We'll talk about it when I get there."

Randall left his house that afternoon, relieved there was no lunch rush waiting for him. He smiled, thinking of the conversation Daniel Lee and Veronica would have. A laugh erupted as he imagined Daniel Lee trying to speak business terms and Veronica wielding her ghetto gibberish. It would take them at least an hour to reach an agreement and he laughed, until he thought of his son. He'd made the same fatal farewell as she had. *I'm coming right back.*

There were more visions of horrible endings for his son as he made his way onto Memorial Drive. Maybe that junk car had failed him on a desolate road somewhere and he'd been abducted trying to get help. Maybe he'd headed for Texas but never made it, setting up camp somewhere west of Georgia. Then

Randall had the most peculiar thought. Corey had gone to find her. He wanted something new. Perhaps they had been communicating for weeks, months — even years. She'd told him the best way to get out was the way she had. Just leave. No explanation, just leave.

His musings were disrupted by a car behind him blowing a high pitched horn. Randall glanced in the rearview mirror as the driver tossed gestures toward him, indicating that the light had long ago changed. He punched the gas, jetting the car along and gaining distance on the Culture Complex billboard. As he drove by the parking lot he noticed the cars filling up spaces as they did every day. He drove further and witnessed a depressing sight that was growing larger every week.

Soul Food Delight-Closed
Waldenbooks- Closed
Nikki's Nails-Closed
Olive Garden-Closed
Trina's Beauty Supply-Closed
Chili's-Closed
Way Out Wings-Closed
Steak and Ale-Closed
Jamar's Clothing-Closed
Po' Folks Cooking- Closed
Sandra's Salon-Closed
Kroger-Closed
Soul Style Barber Shop-Closed
Community Business Center-Closed

His community was being consumed and he couldn't slay the monster. At first he believed crime was the dragon that was setting businesses on fire. Then he thought it was the change in demographics. Once upon a time he theorized that it was the recycling of the community's own spending. Finally, he tried to face the reality of businesses like his own being poorly managed. He concluded that there wasn't one beast to slay, but several creatures of doom that had to be defeated. His community didn't have an army big enough to win.

"Hey, Detective. Got your message. So you got a suspect, one of 'em at least," Randall said, smiling, shaking the detective's hand. He'd met Randall at the entrance and showed him back to the holding area. There was a puzzled look on the detective's face.

"You did get my message I left, right?" asked Detective Askew.

"Yeah, I did and I thank you for doing such good job on this case. I called you back, but I decided to come on down here and take care of it in person. Can you help me with it?"

"With what? I'm sorry I didn't get a chance to check my messages," the detective said, thinking that the stress had finally overtaken Randall and he was delusional.

"You know, Corey. My oldest boy. I wanted to do a missing persons on him. I think he's all right. His brother's passin', ya know, he just need some time to heal. It's really my daughter that's worried sick. Is it a form I need to fill out or something? Can you help me push it through?"

"Mr. Harvey...could you come with me for a moment?" the detective asked, escorting him to a room with an officer guarding it. "I've got it," the detective said to the officer. With a bowed head, he opened the door, and extended his hand as a gesture for Randall to walk in. Randall was deadened by the sight. Sitting in jail clothes, handcuffed to the table, was Corey.

"What the hell is this?" Randall asked, looking at Corey then back at the detective. What the hell is goin' on? Corey, why you in here? We been lookin' for you son. What's wrong, Detective, why y'all got my boy in these chains? Detective, what the hell is this?"

"Pops." Corey said with a dry mouth. He'd refused to speak with anyone and hadn't muttered a word until now. "Pops."

"What wrong, son? Talk to me." Randall fell into the chair across from his son.

"I been tryin' to," he said, sadly. "I been tryin' to talk to you, Pops."

"I know son, I'm right here wit chu now. Tell me what's wrong," Randall said, holding Corey's hands

and trying to ignore the punishing cold steel re-
straining his firstborn. He rubbed his head the way he
had after school. He placed a hand on his shoulder
the way he had after disappointment.

"Ain't no way we would have made it."

"Made what, son? What you talkin' about?"

"We ain't as hungry as they are. We been spoiled. We
got it too good. We came over here on a crowded boat
fightin' the masters to take us back. They came over
here on a crowed boat fightin' the wind to get them
here as fast as they could. They sleep on top of each
other and we can't sleep in the same room. They hungrier than we are, Pops. When you hungry, you'll do
whatever it takes to get a crumb. They ain't just eatin'
crumbs, they stackin' they crumbs in a corner and
puttin' 'em together. Now they got smorgasbords."

"Corey what is you talkin' about? Who is they.
Why are you—"

"All of 'em, that's who. Asians, Mexicans, Indians,
anybody comin' now is hungry. Hungrier than we
ever been and they gon' run us out. Run us out of
business. Run me out of business. That place was
mine, Pops. I had ideas for the restaurant, you know I
got ideas. Ideas ain't nothin' if I ain't got nothin' to
work wit'. You wasn't lookin' at the books, Pops. But
we was losin' mo' money every month. And we
started losin' money a month after they opened up.
They was takin' *my* money. That was *my* money from
the restaurant that *I* was gon' run. Those was gonna
be *my* franchises. So what if I'm selfish. That's the

way I am. I don't know why but that's just me. But they was gon' close *my* restaurant. One way or another they was gon' close it.

"I promise you. I was just tryin' to make 'em sick."

"What?"

"Pops, I wasn't tryin' to kill nobody, I was just tryin' to make 'em sick. Get back some of my business. I swear I wasn't tryin' to kill nobody — "

"Corey, what you tryin' to say! Boy, what you tellin' me? You not sayin' that... I know you ain't!" Randall jumped from the table, towering over him. He turned to the detective, looking for answers. "What is he sayin'?"

"Mr. Harvey, I'm afraid that one of the men in the video tape we received was your son, Corey. He's being charged with manslaughter. I'm sorry."

About the Author

Brian Egeston lives in Georgia where he spends his time writing, thinking about writing, and longing to write. He lives with his incredible and lovely wife, Latise. He welcomes your comments via e-mail sent to brian@brianwrites.com. Also visit his website at:

www.brianwrites.com

Discussion Guide

Carter-Krall Publishing believes that books make people talk and when people talk, the world learns about different cultures, thereby enhancing our existence. Included here is a discussion guide for your reading group, book club, classroom, or general gathering. We hope you'll enjoy the topics listed here and even derive some interesting ones of your own.

1. In the opening scene, at La Familia's, a description is given about pictures on the wall. What do these pictures indicate about owners of the establishment?

2. Randall Harvey tries to solicit extra help from Karen Batch after the first meeting has concluded. Does this show signs of his character or his determination to accomplish a task?

3. Despite the overwhelming feedback from customers, why did Randall continue to allow Veronica to hold her position at Fish Nets?

4. Why was Randall unable to convince Veronica that she desperately needed a change in attitude?

5. After the food poisoning outbreak, it seems that the media and people in the community have placed the blame on Juan Santos. Why is this?

6. What is symbolic about the term and the book title Catfish Quesadillas?

7. Corey, Randall Harvey's oldest son, is enthusiastic about his own business ideas, but none of them seem to pan out. Is this because of the example Randall has set or because of the business environment in his community?

8. Discuss the appearance and mannerisms of the employees at:

   1. The oil change franchise.
   2. The beauty salon.
   3. McDonald's where Karen stopped for a sandwich.

What affect do the characteristics of employees have on customers?

9. Did Juan Santos' and Juliet Lee's business remain successful because they were better at running a company or because they were hungrier for opportunities?

10. When Juan discovers one of the perpetrators is his former employee, why does he let the man decide his own fate?

11. Randall Harvey was a single father and entrepreneur who raised three children into their adulthood. How did this affect his life and business?

12. How do foreign citizens rise to success by operating businesses geared specifically toward other cultures such as nail salons and ethnic restaurants?

13. Why are some cultures offended when this happens?

14. Did Karen Batch regret her involvement with the grant award? Did her move to Oklahoma help her escape the feelings she may have had surrounding the after affects?

15. Discuss the author's comparisons of the different cultures in the story and how they relate to today's society. Were the comparisons accurate? Where they embellished to help with the theme of the book?

16. Discuss what consumers can do to help businesses better serve their community.

Introducing the Brian Buy-Back

Dear Readers,

Being a stickler for customer service myself, it has occurred to me that we must all do our part to insure the best possible satisfaction on behalf of consumers. Therefore, I'd like to make you a special offer. If you purchase any book that I've written and you don't enjoy the story, I'll buy it back from you or give you another one of my books for free.

All you have to do is send me a letter or an e-mail stating what about the story you did not enjoy, a receipt showing the purchase, and the book.

It's not a gimmick, but a gesture of confidence and the ultimate offer of reader appreciation. This offer is good for every book I have written and every book that I'll write for the rest of my life.

Written With Warmth &
Sincerely Scribed,

Brian Egeston

Brian@brianwrites.com
Send Books to:
Carter-Krall Publishing Order Fulfillment
P.O. Box 1388
Pine Lake, GA 30072

Carter-Krall Publishing

Carter-Krall Publishing
Changing the world a word at a time.

☐ **Whippins, Switches & Peach Cobbler**
$13.00 Trade paperback ISBN-096755021
Please send_____ copies.

☐ **♣ ♠♣♣♠♠**
$13.00 Trade paperback ISBN-0967550580
Please send_____copies.

☐ *Catfish Quesadillas*
$13.00 Trade paperback ISBN 0-9675505-5-6
Please send _____ copies.

☐ **The Big Money Match**
$13.00 Trade paperback ISBN 0-9675505-6-4
Please send _____ copies.

Available at your local bookstore or use this page to reorder.
Make check or money order payable to: **Carter-Krall Publishers**
GA residents add 6% sales tax.
MAIL TO:
Carter-Krall Publishers Order Fulfillment Dept.
P.O. Box 1388
Pine Lake, GA 30072

Please send me the items I have checked above. I am enclosing $ _____
(please add $2.15 per book for postage and handling).
Name _____ e-mail _____
Address _____
City/State _____ Zip _____
Please charge my Visa/MC/American Express # _____
Exp. Date _____ Signature _____

Carter-Krall Publishing

Carter-Krall Publishing
Changing the world a word at a time.

☐ **Whippins, Switches & Peach Cobbler**
$13.00 Trade paperback ISBN-096755021
Please send _____copies.

☐   ♣ ♠♠♣♠♠
$13.00 Trade paperback ISBN-0967550580
Please send _____copies.

☐ *Catfish Quesadillas*
$13.00 Trade paperback ISBN 0-9675505-5-6
Please send _____ copies.

☐ **The Big Money Match**
$13.00 Trade paperback ISBN 0-9675505-6-4
Please send _____ copies.

Available at your local bookstore or use this page to reorder.
Make check or money order payable to: **Carter-Krall Publishers**
GA residents add 6% sales tax.

MAIL TO:
Carter-Krall Publishers Order Fulfillment Dept.
P.O. Box 1388
Pine Lake, GA 30072

Please send me the items I have checked above. I am enclosing $ _____
(please add $2.15 per book for postage and handling).
Name _____ e-mail _____
Address _____
City/State _____ Zip _____
Please charge my Visa/MC/American Express # _____
Exp. Date _____ Signature _____

Carter-Krall Publishing

Carter-Krall Publishing
Changing the world a word at a time.

☐ **Whippins, Switches & Peach Cobbler**
$13.00 Trade paperback ISBN-096755021
Please send_____ copies.

☐ **♣ ♠♠♣♠♠**
$13.00 Trade paperback ISBN-0967550580
Please send _____copies.

☐ *Catfish Quesadillas*
$13.00 Trade paperback ISBN 0-9675505-5-6
Please send _____ copies.

☐ **The Big Money Match**
$13.00 Trade paperback ISBN 0-9675505-6-4
Please send _____ copies.

Available at your local bookstore or use this page to reorder.
Make check or money order payable to: **Carter-Krall Publishers**
GA residents add 6% sales tax.
MAIL TO:
Carter-Krall Publishers Order Fulfillment Dept.
P.O. Box 1388
Pine Lake, GA 30072

Please send me the items I have checked above. I am enclosing $ _____
(please add $2.15 per book for postage and handling).
Name _____ e-mail _____
Address _____
City/State _____ Zip _____
Please charge my Visa/MC/American Express # _____
Exp. Date _____ Signature _____